Nicholas Ryan

Copyright © 2014 Nicholas Ryan

This book is dedicated to a fine man: Jim Gilchrist.

I would also like to make special mention of my friend Mike Maynard who has served as beta reader, military advisor, language consultant and zombie technical advisor.

Chapter One.

It was Clinton Harrigan who heard it first – but I wasn't particularly surprised. It was always the devout Christian who seemed to catch the slightest, softest sounds on the air. I had been nodding drowsily in the corner of the room reading by the pale flickering light of a candle when I saw the big red-headed man lower his bible and sit motionless, as though God was whispering in his ear. Then, quite deliberately, he carefully folded down a corner of the page he was reading and tucked the little book back into the pocket of his pants. He heaved himself up from the sofa and went to the window across the room, pressing his face close to the heavy curtain, his eyes vacant and remote. The big man listened for long silent seconds and then turned back to me.

"Helicopter," he said.

I sat up urgently. "Helicopter? Are you sure?"

Harrigan's expression remained as impassive as a carved block of granite. "I'm sure." He ran a meaty hand through the red curls of his hair and even in the gloom of guttering candlelight, I could see the steady glint in the gaze of the man's eyes. "It's coming closer. Still a long way off, but definitely coming closer. Come and listen."

I pushed myself out of the chair and went towards the window.

In the twenty-three days since the zombie apocalypse had devastated the United States, the sounds of military defiance had become less with every passing day. In the first week, the army had been on the streets, and the sound of gunfire roared through the night. Aircraft streaked high overhead, and vapor trails criss-crossed the blue sky as air force jets flew missions further to the north. But as the days had become weeks, the sounds of resistance had grown less frequent, and less determined; like the gasps of a strangling man, choking on his last few precious shallow breaths.

I went quietly across the room and Harrigan stood aside. I twitched the heavy curtains an inch apart, and turned my head. I felt the cool of the night air radiating through the glass.

From the corner of my eye, I saw Jed appear in the doorway that divided the room from the tiny kitchen. He had a cold can of beans in his hand, scooping the food into his mouth with his fingers. He leaned casually against the door-frame, his eyebrows raised in a silent question, but his attitude unreadable.

I turned back to where Harrigan stood.

"I don't hear anything."

"Wait," Harrigan said. "The sound is drifting on the wind. It comes and goes. Be patient."

I frowned, and wondered vaguely what the sound of an approaching helicopter might mean for the three of us. Did it mean the military were back on the offensive? Was this the start of a concerted effort to win back the south-east of the country? Or was it an evacuation? Was the helicopter a last desperate flight to freedom before the entire country was over-run? What sort of helicopter could it be? Maybe it was transporting supplies and equipment. Maybe it was on a reconnaissance mission. The questions and possibilities were impossible to stop – and equally impossible to answer.

Then I heard the sound for myself. My eyes flashed with recognition. God alone knew why a helicopter would be flying over this desolate little town in the middle of rural Virginia – let alone flying at all. We hadn't seen a single sign of life in over a week; man woman or child. So a helicopter was cause for hope – and utter confused incredulity.

"You hear it now, right?" Harrigan asked grimly.

I nodded, my ears straining to keep the ethereal vague sound in contact as it eddied on the night air. "I hear it," I whispered.

Harrigan looked satisfied. His face was a craggy collection of features that had been assembled with no real care. His nose was the shape of a ripe plum, and laced with the tell-tale veins of a man who had once been a heavy drinker. His eyes were dark little things that seemed to get lost between the pale flesh of his cheeks, and the overhanging ridge of his brow. He went to the next window in the room and leaned close.

"It's definitely coming closer," Harrigan announced softly after another brief silent pause. "But it doesn't sound right. It sounds to me like there's something wrong. The turbine – it sounds – irregular."

I couldn't hear any of that. All I could hear was the very distant thump of a helicopter, the sound without any definition, or any sense of its location.

But I didn't doubt Harrigan's judgment. I turned around and stared at Jed.

"It might be military," I said.

Jed pushed himself casually away from the door and left the empty can of beans on a side-table. He wiped his hands on the front of his denim jacket and then dragged the sleeve across his mouth. He winced suddenly, and then said, "So."

"So it might be a way out for us."

Jed grunted, and then belched. He got the taste of it on his breath before he went on. "And it might not." He folded his arms across his chest and stood like a big muscled-bouncer in the middle of the living room floor. There was a sour, bitter look on his face. Then he scratched the bristled stubble of his beard, and winced again. The whole left side of his face was terribly swollen, distorting his features and pulling the skin tight around a lump that reached from his cheek, all the way to under his jawbone. "Unless it lands on the road right outside the door."

I turned my head and pressed my ear back close to the window. The sound was still there – and maybe it was a little louder now – a little more detailed. I thought I could hear the clatter of the rotors as they beat on the dark night air. The sound became clear for a second – and then was washed away.

"Wind?"

Harrigan nodded. "There's a storm on the way," he said. "I can feel it. And you can see the wind through the trees out on the sidewalk." He pointed through the crack in the curtains. I looked out into the blackness through the window in front of me. The shapes of the night were apparitions – everything turned into a nightmare by the ghostly light of a thin slice of moon and wind-swept black clouds that scudded across the stars. The path from the front door was a vague silhouette, but beyond the fence, I could see nothing. Absolutely nothing at all. The night was a dark zombie terror, filled with fear and death that marauded through the blood-drenched streets of America like packs of predatory animals.

"The engine sounds okay to me," I turned back to Harrigan and screwed up my face.

"Me too," Jed said suddenly from behind us. He had his face lifted up to the ceiling, his head tilted to the side, like he was inspecting the paint and plaster work. Then he made a long explosive hacking sound, and hawked a glob of green slimy phlegm onto the carpet. He winced again.

I watched as Jed carefully pulled one of his last precious cigarettes from a crumpled pack in his coat pocket and lit it. He inhaled a lungful of smoke and breathed out a cloud of blue haze with a contented sigh. "Sounds like any other helicopter."

Harrigan shot Jed a malevolent glare, and then he turned back to face me. "It's not," Harrigan said with absolute conviction. "Mitch, the helicopter has some kind of engine trouble – and it seems to be coming closer. And lower."

"Circling?"

Harrigan shook his head. "I don't think so. But maybe."

"Looking for something?"

"Perhaps. Or looking for a safe place to land."

Behind me, I heard Jed hiss. "You're fucking kidding," he snorted derisively. "First, what makes you so sure the helicopter is in trouble, big-boy? It sounds perfectly normal to me. And," he stabbed a finger at Harrigan like he was thrusting with a pointed blade, "what makes you so sure it is dropping lower, or looking for a place to land? Did God tell you that? Did you just get the word from the Big Guy in the sky?"

Harrigan's lips drew into a thin bloodless grimace, and bit down on his frustration. His policy of turning the other cheek left him an easy target for ridicule. It had been the same from the moment the quiet gentle man had appeared outside the house a week before, covered in someone else's blood, his eyes wild and crazed with terror as he had pounded on the front door and pleaded for shelter.

"I lived near an executive airport in South Carolina for three years," Harrigan said with measured restraint. "I know."

I shot Jed a glare meant to urge him into silence. He ignored me. He took a step closer to Harrigan and reached for the Glock that was tucked inside his belt.

Jed was a big man – a huge, muscled giant. He was the kind of man who had always gotten what he wanted by the sheer size and weight of his presence. He was like a man-mountain of pumped, buffed muscle. He was three inches taller than me, and fifty pounds heavier. His chest and arms were covered in awkward tattoos that rose all the way up to his neck. And there were scars. Ones he had never told me about, but ones he didn't need to talk about either. They criss-crossed the bridge of his nose and the broad flat of his forehead. He was a one-man muscled wall of violent destruction, unhindered by conscience, reason or logic.

He was my younger brother, and he had done time.

Hard time.

"You religious bastards are all the same," Jed chambered a round into the Glock and glanced down at the weapon casually as he spoke. He used the short barrel of the gun to scratch under his chin. "You think God is going to save you, even when you're standing knee deep in a living hell," Jed said. His words were slightly slurred. If there had been beer left in the house, I would have thought him drunk, but I knew it was the terrible pain of an infected tooth that was distorting the sound of his words. In a strange way, the slur seemed to add menace. I felt myself bracing. It wouldn't be the first time in the last week the two men before me had been on the brink of a confrontation. I could see it in Jed's eyes; he wasn't used to anyone challenging him, or questioning him. Harrigan's stoic, resolute quiet confidence rattled and unnerved my brother in a way he wasn't sure how to deal with.

Harrigan stared, and then turned his back without a word. At first I thought he was deliberately provoking Jed into violence – but then I realized it was the sound of the approaching helicopter that compelled his attention. All of a sudden the roar of the rotors was like a deafening thunder that sounded as if it were directly overhead.

I looked up in sudden alarm. I could feel the force of the noise and tremendous downdraft of the rotors seem to shake and beat at the building. The windows rattled in their casements and the floor beneath my feet seemed to shudder. I saw Harrigan press his face close to the window again, his eyes narrowed slits against the night.

He was waiting.

I stared up at the ceiling. The roar of the helicopter rose to a swelling thunder – and then it was past us – seemingly flying directly over the rooftop. It was low. The sound was deafening. The air shuddered, and over the scythe of the huge rotors, I could hear the high-pitched whine of the turbine.

I heard Harrigan shout, and I snapped my eyes to where he stood at the window.

"It's searching for something," Harrigan confirmed, still with his face pressed hard against the glass. "He's using a spotlight."

I dashed to a window, but in the instant of time it took me, the helicopter had already flashed out of sight, disappearing behind the trees and houses on the opposite side of the road. The clattering avalanche of noise began to fade as the rising wind tore the reverberating sound to shreds.

I turned to Harrigan. "What did you see?"

"It may be military, but I don't think so," he said carefully, as though he were assembling his thoughts as he spoke. "The shape seemed to be more commercial – like a Bell JetRanger. But it was painted a flat dark color." He screwed up his face like he was dealing with a particularly puzzling problem. "Like a night-flying camouflage."

That made no sense.

"That makes no sense," I said. "Why camouflage a helicopter from prying eyes. There are no prying eyes – everyone is dead, or undead. They could paint it bright pink with yellow flowers. The point is – who are they hiding from?"

Harrigan had no answer – because there was no answer.

"Did you hear the turbine?" he asked me.

I nodded.

"It was straining –almost like the pilot was using every ounce of power just to keep the thing in the air," Harrigan said. He huffed, and chewed his bottom lip for a moment. "I think the pilot is looking for a place to crash land, Mitch. I think he's got to set it down before it falls from the sky. That's why the spotlight was on. He's looking for somewhere to land."

My God.

I stared back out through the window. I couldn't see the helicopter, but I could still hear the roar of the rotors. But what I was visualizing then was not the helicopter – I was seeing the pilot, hunched over the controls and desperately struggling to keep the ungainly bird in the air. Were there passengers? How many? I couldn't possibly guess – but I could imagine the moment when the helicopter finally lost its fight to fly and fell in a screaming horror to the ground. If the pilot lost power before setting down, the impact of the collision could be catastrophic; tearing the rotors from the helicopter and shattering them into a thousand scything blades as the metal shell around the man crumpled, and he sat dazed and dying harnessed into his seat...

The clatter of the helicopter's percussive beat came again, louder for an instant and then fading once more, like a punch of violent sound. I turned away from the window and stared into Harrigan's eyes.

"Did you hear that?" he asked me.

I nodded. "I heard it."

"He's trying to land. The sound isn't fading anymore. It's constant, and he's not too far away – somewhere beyond those houses across the street."

I figured as much. I visualized the helicopter, rocking and pitching a hundred feet above the ground as the pilot juggled the controls and tried to find a clear area to land. In my mind's eye I saw a console of flashing indicator lights, buzzing emergency alarms, and a man perhaps only moments from death.

"Thoughts?"

Harrigan rubbed hard at his face, like he was trying to rearrange his features to create something more handsome, and then he sighed heavily. "I think we should."

I nodded. "I think so too."

I spun on my heel, filled with sudden tense energy. Jed was standing right behind me. I brushed past him and reached for the black nylon bag that was on the sofa. It was packed with spare ammunition for the Glocks, and some of the emergency supplies I had been able to throw together before the world went to hell in a hand-basket. The bag wasn't very heavy.

"We're going to rescue the pilot," I said calmly. I slung the strap of the bag over my shoulder and checked the Glock tucked down inside the waistband of my jeans to make sure the magazine was full.

For long seconds Jed's face remained blank and impassive – and then the realization struck him.

"Like hell," he snapped, suddenly bristling with defiant outrage. "I'm not going anywhere." His eyes were wide and wild.

I shrugged. "Suit yourself," I said. "But that doesn't change anything. Harrigan and I are going."

"Jesus!" Jed growled from the center of the room. "Are you out of your mind? Even if the pilot lands that thing, he's still dead, Mitch. Every zombie within ten miles is going to be drawn to the sound of the helicopter. They'll be all over him. Whether he survives the crash or not – he's still dead."

I threw a couple of empty plastic water bottles into the bag, and snatched my leather jacket off the back of the chair. Harrigan was shrugging on a long heavy overcoat.

"You're probably right," I said to Jed. "But we're still going."

"Then you're dead."

I shrugged. "Maybe," I agreed. "But so are you."

He bristled, and shook his head. Jed wasn't the sharpest tool in the shed. Sometimes things took a little longer to register – and sometimes things needed to be explained.

"What do you mean by that? I told you I ain't going with you."

I let the bag slide off my shoulder and I sighed. "Jed, we're just about out of food. There's maybe enough water for another day or two, but after that… nothing. If we stay here, we're going to die. If we make a break for it, we're going to die – because we don't know where any other survivors are. We've been isolated for over three weeks. So either way, you're a dead man if you stay here."

Jed frowned. I let my words sink in. "This pilot is our only hope," I explained patiently. "If we find him, and if he's alive, he'll know where other survivors are. Based on the direction the helicopter flew in, he has come from somewhere north of here – and he's in a helicopter. That means civilization still exists – somewhere. He's our only chance of getting through this nightmare. So we have to go out and try to save him – because we're trying to save ourselves, *you dumb ignorant, stupid bastard.*"

Jed flinched. I saw angry color rising in his one good cheek, and his eyes narrowed until they were dark and dangerous.

"What did you call me?" his voice rumbled.

Behind Jed's back, Clinton Harrigan picked up his heavy crowbar and hefted it in his hand. He looked me a silent question with undisguised relish.

I shook my head – a sharp curt gesture. "I called you a dumb. ignorant bastard," I answered Jed. "You think this is some heroic good-

Samaritan gesture? You think I want to go out into the night – and into a storm – to find a crashed helicopter, knowing there's maybe only a ten percent chance the pilot is alive? Jesus, Jed!" I snapped. "This is our best chance to save ourselves. Do I care about the pilot? Not really. What I care about is living through this apocalypse and I know that if we stay here we're going to die – either from starvation, or from being forced to make a crazy escape with no idea where we are going, and no way of getting there."

For long seconds, the air in the room crackled with tension, and then Jed seemed to deflate. The bluster went out of him and he slumped his shoulders and prodded absently at his swollen cheek with his fingers. "Are we coming back here?" he asked at last. His voice was a flat, heavy monotone.

I shook my head. "I doubt it," I said. "There's nothing to come back for. If the pilot is alive, and if he was flying towards a specific location, then most probably it's to the south of here because that's the course he was flying. There's no point rescuing him and doubling back to this place. We'll find another safe place to spend the night, and then work out a plan in the morning."

"If we survive until then," Jed said gloomily.

I nodded. "If we survive until then."

We weren't well armed. Jed and I had Glock's and a few boxes of ammunition to share between us. Harrigan didn't have a gun. He had a crowbar. He reminded me of Friar Tuck from the Robin Hood legend – a big beefy holy man who somehow believed guns to be dangerous – but had no problem with cleaving the iron forked claw of a crowbar down into the skull of an undead attacker.

We went through the house quickly. I stuffed a blanket into the bag, and the last few cans of beans from the kitchen. There was enough water to fill half-a-dozen plastic drink bottles, so we dumped them into the nylon bag, and Jed filled his pockets with the boxes of ammunition for the guns to lighten the load.

We stood in the center of the living room floor like a trio of strangers waiting for a train, checking over each other's preparations. Harrigan's jacket was one of those long black woolen pieces that reached all the way down to his knees. It was thick and warm. He turned the collar up and rolled his shoulders as he took a test-swing with the crowbar. Jed's denim jacket had some kind of gang colors on the back. He buttoned it up to his throat and forced a tight strained smile.

My leather jacket was an old black thing I'd owned for years. It was like me – worn around the edges. But it was thick. It would give me protection against random bites, but just to be certain, I wrapped some shredded lengths of torn linen bedsheet up to the elbow of my left arm to give me added protection. Jed saw what I was doing and thought it was a good idea. He did the same. Then there was nothing more to do – except step out into the night and put our lives on the line.

* * *

The front door was bolted, and I had hammered four-inch nails into the frame during the first terrifying days of the zombie apocalypse. So we assembled in the small kitchen at the rear of the house. The back door had been chained, and we had heaved the refrigerator across the entry as a barricade.

I stood with my back against the door and unfastened the latch. Jed stole a glance through the kitchen window and gave me the 'thumbs-up' sign.

We had survived for three weeks through good luck and stealth. Every window in the house had been kept curtained. The doors had been bolted and blockaded. We burned one candle in the evening – and we stayed quiet. It had kept us alive. In the first few days of terror, the streets had been a screaming nightmare of endless terror and unspeakable horrors. The gutters ran with blood as the infection spread across the town. We had avoided death by avoiding being noticed.

Now we were about to step out into a world we didn't know any more. I was scared.

I cracked the door open and stood for a long moment, scanning the darkness for an immediate sign of danger. A gust of sweet, cold fresh air slapped me in the face and my eyes watered. The air in the house was smoky and stale with the odor of sweat and fear. Suddenly I was keen to be clear of the place.

I pulled the back door open and stepped quietly out into the night. A flagstone path ran from the back door, around the side of the house to the driveway. I went along the path for a dozen paces and then stopped. I looked behind me and could see Jed standing in the doorway, watching me. I went down on one knee and waved to him. He came out through the door and crept to where I waited. I could hear him breathing, the sound of it rasping and loud. He had his Glock in his hand, swinging it in an arc of about ninety degrees towards the back fence.

It was a small yard with a child's swing set and a couple of stunted trees near the back fence. The grass had grown long and become choked with weeds. Jed swept his gun from side to side, as though he expected the dark gnarled trees to come alive.

I waved to Harrigan. He came out through the door, and left it swinging open. He scuffled to where I was kneeling. There was an urgent look in his eyes. I pressed my mouth close to his ear and whispered.

"What's wrong?"

"The sound of the helicopter has changed again. Can you hear it?"

I frowned. We were protected from the wind by the bulk of the house so that the sound was just background noise, overlaid by the distant, steady beat of the helicopter's rotors. I shook my head. "Sounds the same to me," I said. "Sounds like he's still hovering, maybe."

"But it's moved," Harrigan said in an impatient whisper. "It's coming from further east, like he's still looking for a place to set down."

I frowned again and listened harder, trying to isolate the noise of the chopper. The thumping beat of the helicopter surged and receded as the wind came in gusts and then fell away, like the crash of surf on the shoreline. Maybe Harrigan was right... or maybe it was the wind that was changing direction as the impending storm swept closer to the town.

A rent of lightning ripped across the sky, and I looked up. Beyond the silhouette of distant dark trees, I saw the lingering flash backlight banks of dark ugly storm clouds. I got to my feet and tightened my grip on the Glock.

I reached the corner of the house and glanced behind me. Harrigan was at my shoulder, and Jed was close behind him. We stood in a tight knot just long enough for me to take a single deep breath and crush down on my fear and panic.

I stepped around the side of the house and into the teeth of the rising wind.

I wasn't prepared. The wind was demonic: a howling gusting blast of cold damp air that punched at my body and forced me to slit my eyes tight. The air was full of leaves and debris and dirt. I hunched my shoulders and threw my free hand up in front of my face.

The driveway ran the length of the house and ended at a mailbox. I covered the distance as quickly as I could. The night was utterly dark. Storm clouds had overwhelmed the moon.

When I got to the mailbox I glanced both ways along the street. The night was like a cloak, hiding the debris of crashed cars, smashed windows, overgrown lawns and burned, blackened buildings. But the darkness also hid the deadly danger of marauding zombies that I knew must be lurking in the night.

I turned my back to the teeth of the driving wind and hunched deeper into the warmth of my leather jacket.

"Across the street," I said over the moaning wail of the wind. Harrigan nodded. Jed did the same. I turned back around and – before I had time to change my mind – I broke into a sprint.

The wind punched at me as I broke from the last illusions of protective cover. It was swirling between the buildings, driving a skirt of biting dust and dirt before it. I felt the strength of it push me sideways and tug at my body. I squinted my eyes and looked up into the night, scanning the sky above the dark shape of the roofline ahead. I caught a quick glimpse of the helicopter's spotlight, wavering like a strobe in the distance. It was ahead, and further to my left. I made a mental note of its approximate location in the sky – and then it was gone completely – either obscured by the height of the houses I was running towards, or because the pilot had dipped so low to the ground that the spotlight was blocked from view.

Or because the chopper had fallen from the sky and crashed.

No. It hadn't done that. Not yet at least. I could still hear the rhythmic *thump-thump-thump* of the rotors, beating against the wind. The sound of it became louder, and then just as quickly faded again.

I ran on, feeling hopelessly exposed and vulnerable. It was just twenty feet to the opposite side of the road and the shelter of the houses there – but it was the longest few seconds of my life. My arms pumped, and my chest heaved like a billows. The nylon bag was slung from my shoulders. It thumped against my back as I moved.

I leaped the gutter and landed badly. I felt my left leg go from under me and then I was falling. I went down in soft grass, my momentum hurling me end over end until I felt cold concrete under my back. I got up quickly and checked myself for injury. My legs were trembling and the surging adrenalin made my hands shake. I stood gingerly and took a couple of steps.

Nothing broken. Nothing sprained.

The night was so dark that it was impossible to see more than a few feet in front of my hands. There was no ambient light. There was no light at all. I heard my brother's heavy footsteps as he pounded across the blacktop and then he was rasping and gasping for breath beside me. Harrigan came across the street last. He was a big beefy man. I didn't imagine he would be fast on his feet. I heard him well before I saw him – heard his ragged gasping breath as he came closer. He must have been running with his arms outstretched because I felt the slap of his palm against my shoulder as he almost crashed into me.

We didn't wait.

A dark solid shape loomed ahead of us – the silhouette of a house. I knew this place because I had stared anxiously through the curtains a hundred times in the past few weeks, scouring the neighborhood for marauding zombies. It was a two-story home, directly across the road from the house we had been hiding in. I remembered there was a row of low hedges that served as a fence-line across the front of the property, and I groped my way forward until I felt the brush of small leaves and branches. I kept my hand extended, and began to pace tentatively until I came to a break in the foliage. I felt more concrete under my feet – the path that led down the side of the house. I turned and waited for Jed and Harrigan to find me. It took a moment. We were like three blind men, the task made all the more difficult by the howling wind that moaned and shrieked like some mournful lament of the damned.

And maybe that's what we were.

"Stick close," I pressed my mouth close to Jed's ear. "Keep each other in sight."

I went along the path, and sensed the shape of the house overhanging us like an avalanche of black. The path was narrow, and I kept my hands outstretched, feeling my way. The path was flat. I could feel long grass and low scrubby thorns snagging at my jeans. I pushed on, moving in a cautious crouch as we suddenly walked into a hole in the wind.

We were walking close against the side of the house. The building was buffering the force of the gale. We could still hear it howling through the trees and rooftops, but suddenly it was calm enough that I could open my eyes fully and rub the grit and dirt from them. I took a chance.

"Jed, give me your lighter."

I needed to get my bearings. I knew where we were – but I had no idea what lay beyond. The view of this house from the living room window of our hideout showed this path that lead down the side of the home... but then what?

I sensed Jed rustling through his pockets, and then felt him press the cigarette lighter into the palm of my hand. We crouched down, making ourselves as small a target as possible and I flicked the lighter. I cupped my hand around the tiny orange glow. It threw off just enough light for me to see the faded green clapboard siding of the house, a few feet of concrete path – and Jed and Harrigan's taut, strained faces, cast in a ghostly orange glow that deepened the shadows of their features so they looked like undead apparitions.

The glow from the lighter also turned every tree, hedge and fern into ghastly nightmarish shapes. I flicked the lighter off.

"I think this path leads all the way around to the rear of the house," I whispered. Jed and Harrigan leaned closer. "There has to be a back fence. We find it, and we go over it. It's our best chance of avoiding trouble," I explained, hoping I sounded calm. "The Zed's won't be wandering around suburban back yards in the middle of the night – they'll be roaming the streets – so we stay low and we stay close to cover. Okay?"

I must have sounded confident. Jed and Harrigan simply nodded. Then I felt Harrigan's big meaty hand – a hand the size and shape of a baseball mitt – on my shoulder. "The chopper," he said cautiously. "It's moved again. I think it's coming back this way, Mitch."

I propped my head to the side and tried to focus my attention. The sound of the rotors was still a constant noise, but it had been the same for so long now that I had to focus in order to separate the sound from the undulating howl of the wind that carried it. I shrugged. It didn't sound any different to me, but I wasn't prepared to doubt Harrigan's verdict. "What do you think that means?"

Harrigan was silent for long seconds. "He might not be able to find a safe place to set down," Harrigan speculated. "We're in the suburbs. There are power poles and wires everywhere. Maybe he's trying to use up fuel – like planes do before they crash. They try to burn up fuel, or they dump it to reduce the risk of an explosion." He shrugged again. "All I know for sure is that he's edging his way back towards us."

"He might be circling," Jed offered. "He might be waiting."

No one commented. Jed's words got whipped away by the wind. The truth was – we didn't know.

But we were going to find out.

I got to my feet and cast another glance skyward. The night was a heavy blanket. Somewhere in the sky was the moon – but the banks of storm clouds were so dark and so low to the ground with the weight of pending rain, that not even the faintest night glow seeped through. Nor could I see the helicopter's spotlight. Either the pilot had switched it off – or he was still too low for us to see it.

I took a deep breath. It was cold. I felt the air bite in my lungs, but my body was drenched in a nervous adrenalin-fueled sweat. I could feel the perspiration wet in my hairline and on the back of my neck, trickling down inside my tee-shirt. I wiped my palm on my jeans. The handle of the Glock was slippery and damp. Then I started down the path towards the back fence with Jed and Harrigan shadowing me.

I went slowly – unsure of exactly what I might be walking into, and doing my best to keep the concrete path under my feet as it seemed to meander its way past small gardens and rock features. Then the sky was ripped apart by a jagged blue flash of lightning, and for a split second everything ahead of me was frozen and burned onto my eyes.

There was a retaining wall ahead of us and another garden that fringed the back fence of the property. The fence was made of wooden palings. I went forward slowly.

I waded into a barrier of rose bushes and thorny shrubs, then felt the rough timber of the fence. I crouched down and waited for Harrigan and Jed. The fence gave some shelter from the swirling wind. I could hear it moaning through the tree-tops, and a flurry of leaves rained down on me. Somewhere overhead I heard a branch snap – the sound like the retort of a gunshot.

Jed squatted down in the garden beside me. We waited another minute. Nothing.

Clinton Harrigan had disappeared.

I cursed under my breath. Overhead, thunder rumbled with a sound like artillery fire, and the wind shrieked. There was no point calling out to Harrigan – he wouldn't hear me unless I shouted, and I didn't want to do that.

27

I fumbled Jed's lighter from my pocket and lit it. The glow was a weak puny spark in the impenetrable depth of the night. It cast a small glow that showed me Jed's face and the fence. Nothing more. But I wasn't expecting to miraculously see Harrigan wandering around, lost in the darkness.

I was expecting him to see the glow, like a lighthouse in the middle of the night.

A few moments later I heard him, clambering for a foothold on the retaining wall, and then he was next to me, his breath ragged and his eyes wide and wild with the remnants of his panic.

I felt the big man's weight slump against the fence. "Sorry," he muttered bitterly. "I lost you for a moment. One minute I was following Jed, with my eyes on his back – and the next I was bumping into God-knows what and starting to panic."

I said nothing.

I hadn't been afraid of the dark since I was a kid.

But I was now. The night terrified me. As a child I had believed the darkness was filled with horror and monsters. Then I grew up and realized my fear was merely a child's imagination.

But not now. Now the terror was real. Now the night really was alive with monsters.

And horror.

And death.

Harrigan had been on the verge of blind, terrified panic. I could see that in his eyes, and I could hear it in his voice. And I understood and sympathized.

I slapped him on the back and flicked off the lighter. "It's okay," I said. "From now on, you stay in the middle. Jed, you bring up the rear."

I got to my feet and took a grip on the fence. It must have been old. As I heaved myself up, I felt it begin to sway. I scrambled to the top, and pushed myself out into the dark space – and then realized, too late, that I was a fool. I had no idea what was on this side of the fence. I should have used the lighter again. I should have taken the extra moment to be sure. But I didn't.

For all that I got lucky. I landed on my feet on soft grass. I went down into a crouch and pressed my back against the fence. Another violent rent of lightning tore the night apart and I saw a small clearing and then a patch of light woods. This wasn't someone's back yard. This was some kind of a nature preserve that the developers must have included when the suburb had been built.

I called softly back to Jed and Harrigan, and felt their weight coming onto the fence and then heard them landing on the grass nearby. Harrigan sounded like he was struggling. This was probably more physical activity than he got in a year. It was like taking on an army obstacle course – blindfolded.

I crept forward and found both men a few feet away.

"We've got a strip of grass – maybe thirty feet of clear ground – and then there is a fringe of trees," I explained in a hoarse whisper.

I closed my eyes for a moment and concentrated on the sound of the helicopter. It was closer now. The roar of the rotors seemed to be almost above us. I groped in the darkness until I felt Harrigan's arm and pressed my face close to his.

"I think the helicopter is still on the move."

There was a pause. "Sounds like it," Harrigan agreed. "He's definitely coming back this way. He's definitely doubled back, or he's circling," Harrigan said with absolute confidence. "I think he's lower now. The wind and the storm must be giving him hell."

I thought about that for the first time. Up until now, I had only considered the plight of the pilot from a mechanical prospect; the terror of flying a helicopter that had some kind of mechanical fault, and the fear of crashing. Now I factored in the added danger of keeping an ailing helicopter in the air in the teeth of a howling wind and a night sky full of storm clouds and lightning.

Maybe the helicopter's mechanical problems weren't as severe as we had first imagined.

Or maybe the pilot was far better at his trade than I had ever considered...

I got to my feet and struck out across the open ground, moving in a bent-over crouch, counting my steps. I had guessed there was about thirty feet of open ground to the tree-line, and after twenty paces I paused and took a breath. Harrigan bumped into my back and then stopped.

"What's up?" he whispered.

I didn't answer.

I didn't know. But something other than caution had made me stop. Some instinct perhaps – or some sixth sense. I went perfectly still and my finger curled around the trigger of the Glock.

Without turning my head – and without looking away – I reached behind me and pushed Harrigan back. "Down!" I said urgently.

I stared hard into the darkness before me. I knew the trees were somewhere close ahead, but I had also sensed movement. Maybe it was the trees, bending and swaying before the wind – but I didn't think so. There was something else on the wind – something more than the electricity-charged air of the rising storm.

It was the stench of decay.

My eyes were useless – it was just too damned dark to see anything. I closed them and concentrated.

The wind swirled, and for a moment I could sense and smell nothing other than the heavy perfume of grass and earth. Then the pall of death came again, seeming to rise up from somewhere close ahead of me. I didn't make a sound. I felt a lump of fear choke the breath out of me, and the Glock felt like a lead weight.

Slowly I reached into my pocket for the lighter with my left hand. The seconds dragged on. The rank, decaying smell seemed to coat the back of my mouth so that I felt myself begin to gag. I opened my eyes and stared directly ahead. I could see nothing. I could sense no movement. I tightened my finger on the trigger of the Glock – and struck the lighter.

The flash of orange glow in the night was like a bright, burning flare. Without my free hand shielding the light, the area ahead of us was thrown into dramatic relief.

I stared fixedly ahead, my gun hand extended, my finger tight on the trigger, and my whole body tensed and coiled, expecting violence. I gritted my teeth.

Nothing.

Nothing at all. The night was empty.

I stared, bewildered.

And then I looked down.

There was a young girl's body lying in the grass at my feet. She might have been ten, certainly no older. She was wearing a floral dress. She was lying on her back, one arm flung out, the other still clutching the dirty, muddied shape of a stuffed teddy bear. The girl's face was grey rotting flesh. Her eyes were gone, and the soft alabaster skin of her cheeks was crawling with writhing swarms of maggots. She had been shot once. Through the head. Her hair was crusted stiff with dirt and dried blood. She had been dead for some time.

Rats had gnawed their way through the fabric of her dress and torn the flesh from her abdomen to burrow into her stomach cavity. Ragged swollen entrails lay in the long grass beside her. I felt my stomach heave, and a scalding burn in the back of my throat. I turned to the side and retched.

Sheet lightning jagged across the sky and for an instant everything around us was lit. The trees before us were outlined as stark black shapes below the heavy belly of the storm clouds, and a trick of the sudden light seemed to make the dead girl's body move.

I took a step back.

Then the night slammed down again, plunging the world around us back into solid darkness.

I reeled away from the body, my hands trembling, and a surge of hysterical relieved laughter leaped into my throat.

"You okay?" Harrigan's voice from near by lifted anxiously.

"Yeah," I said, but my voice was shaky. I wiped my mouth with the back of my hand. "There's a dead girl here. She's been dead for a while. I.... I thought I saw her move. It scared me shitless."

There was a rustle of movement from the others, and I heard Jed laugh softly.

I took a deep breath. My mouth was dry, my breathing too quick, and I could feel a flush of warmth beneath the skin of my cheeks from the fright. I cleared my throat. "The trees are just ahead of us," I muttered. "Let's go."

We moved in single file, so close together that I could sense Harrigan's bulky body right behind me. I moved with high, cautious steps, lifting my feet with exaggerated care and placing them gently back into the grass, like a man walking blindly through a minefield. I doubted the girl's body was the only one laying nearby – and maybe the next one we stumbled across would rise up and lunge for us.

We reached the tree line and paused.

I felt the tension rise. It was in all of us. I could hear it in Harrigan's and Jed's breathing, and in their footsteps as we edged our way through the woods. I could feel it in the brush of Harrigan's arm against mine, and in the occasional odor of their bodies that carried in the wind – the scent of anxious sweat and strung-out nerves.

Ahead of us, the heavy cloud bank was beginning to lift, and I could see the first hint of moonlight as it shone through shredded tatters of cloud. It was no longer utterly dark and we moved more quickly. There was a dull orange glow of light reflecting from the belly of the clouds that grew brighter and then faded – then brightened once more. I frowned, and kept my eyes on the clouds until we reached the edge of the trees and stood in a tight knot. I was breathing hard, and drenched in sweat. Not the healthy sweat that comes from strenuous exercise – this was the nervous sweat of someone right on the edge of terror. I could feel my shirt sticking to my back.

I turned to Harrigan and Jed and pointed wordlessly at the clouds. The orange glow was like a pulse of distant flickering light.

"Something's burning," Jed grunted. "Maybe a building. Maybe a whole street," he shrugged. "But it's not nearby. Maybe a mile or two."

I nodded. It made sense. The glow from burning buildings reflected off the low clouds. But I was at least grateful for the light. It was the first lucky break we'd had.

Then it started to rain.

I felt the first fat drops of it splash against my face, and then an instant later the heavens opened up and the rain became a solid downpour – a veil of grey slanting mist that hissed in the trees and soaked us completely.

Ahead of us was another thin strip of long grass and then a suburban street that ran from left to right into the darkness. On the other side of the road was a cluster of one-story neat homes with the dark shapes of abandoned cars on the street and in driveways.

The rain detonated off the blacktop and drummed against the roofs. It crushed down on us like a physical weight and the sky seemed to fill with the boom of thunder that rumbled and rolled across the sky.

I looked up, through the thin canopy of leaves – and then I heard a new, more urgent sound.

The helicopter.

The noise of it was a shrieking assault on the ears.

The helicopter was practically overhead, hanging in the sky. It was swaying from side to side, and the percussive sound as it roared past seemed to undulate as the chopper veered and dipped like flotsam on a storm-tossed angry ocean.

I saw Harrigan's face. I saw his mouth open. I saw him shouting something at me, but I couldn't hear above the roar of the rotors. Then the shape tilted onto its side, and a brilliant bright shaft of light lanced down from the underbelly of the craft, swaying wickedly like a flashlight in the hands of a drunken man.

I felt Jed grip my arm savagely as the helicopter yawed and spun again, seemingly out of control.

Jed crammed his face next to mine. He pointed.

"The house across the street!" he shouted. "He's going to crash right into it!"

We stood, transfixed in horror. The helicopter lifted on a gust of wind, and then plunged back down, dropping dangerously low to sagging power lines. Then it seemed to pivot on its axis and fly directly toward the rooftops of the houses. It dropped like a stone, falling at a sharp angle, its bubbled Perspex nose almost in a vertical dive. I felt myself tense. I felt my body bracing itself for the impact – the shattering, explosive collision as the helicopter disappeared into the building and they both went up in a horrific fireball of death and destruction. The searchlight swayed back and forth, lighting up the house like broad daylight. I saw a porch, entwined with twisted green vines. I saw blank, empty windows, like vacant eyes. I saw a Japanese hatchback hunched low on the driveway – and then I saw the dark twisted shape of a man appear in the open doorway, his head turned up to the night sky, his movements jerky and unnatural – everything cast in brilliant white-light.

The man stumbled out onto the porch. The searchlight swung away haphazardly, and then veered back a moment later. I saw the man moving, alert. The man seemed to snarl up at the sky, his expression crazed and vicious. An instant later we were plunged back into darkness as the spotlight moved away. I felt a sudden sense of fear and alarm. The man was undead – of that I was sure – and he wouldn't be the only ghoul drawn to the rising sound of the helicopter. I tightened my grip on the Glock and took a deep breath. I told myself I had expected this. Finding the helicopter and rescuing the pilot was always going to be a deadly dangerous risk.

But now I wasn't so sure I was prepared for the reality of fighting off the undead, armed with just a couple of pistols and a crow-bar.

I hunted the darkness, my eyes searching the lawns and driveway for any sign of movement, my sense of alarm and unease rising. The man had disappeared.

But to where? He could be anywhere. He could have gone around to the rear of the house – or he could be shambling his way across the street towards me...

The whine of the helicopter's engine tore my attention back up into the night sky. The chopper was plunging towards its destruction.

But at the last possible moment, the helicopter seemed to gather itself like a horse about to meet a fence. It lifted, surged. I heard the engine screaming in protest and the helicopter seemed to hang on its tail, maybe just fifty feet in the air. It went over the roof of the house directly across from where we watched, and then disappeared from sight in a wind-whipped cloud of dust and leaves and rain and noise.

I felt Harrigan beside me, his body brushing past my shoulder as he stepped impulsively out from the shelter of the tree line and into the long grass that fringed the road. "Come on!" he said, his voice a ragged hiss. "He's going down behind that house. We've got to get there– fast!"

I reached for him – too late. In an instant, Harrigan was half-way across the street.

Jesus!

I punched Jed in the shoulder. "Come on!" I said. "But keep your eyes peeled, for God's sake. I saw a zombie come out of the house. It was a man. He could be anywhere."

We went out into the open night, chasing after Harrigan. The big man seemed to have grown wings, moving like an Olympic sprinter. I scrambled in the long grass and muddy ground and then my feet hit the hard surface of the tarmac and I plunged after him. When I knew I couldn't catch him in time, I risked everything – including our lives.

"Wait!" I shouted, knowing that single word would be enough to draw the zombie's unrelenting attention.

Harrigan seemed to freeze in mid-stride. He was standing on the home's front lawn. His body seemed to cringe – as though shocked by the desperation of my cry. He turned, his expression blank, and yet somehow his tension radiated in the way he held his body.

He was suddenly scared.

I ran on towards him, hunched under the driving onslaught of the rain and with the nylon bag pounding against my back and slowing me like an anchor. I heard Jed right behind me, but I didn't take my eyes off Harrigan. As I ran I thrust out my arm.

Harrigan must have thought I was pointing at him. I saw his expression transform into one of bewilderment – and then everything seemed to happen in the blink of an eye.

From behind Harrigan, a ghostly grey shape appeared through the driving curtain of rain. It was a drifting, shambling shadow that attacked from behind the black shape of a garden shrub.

The zombie lunged at Harrigan. I saw its face become a twisted mask of rage. I saw its undead eyes widen. I saw the dark blood that streaked the ghoul's shirt, and the fingers – seized into claws as it struck.

Obliterated by the sound of the storm, and the desperate whine of the helicopter's rotors, the zombie's attack was silent. Its mouth was open – maybe it was growling. Maybe there was a blood-curdling roar in the back of its throat. I heard nothing of it – and I was certain Harrigan would hear nothing either.

I wasn't pointing as I ran. I had the Glock in my hand, arm extended, and I squeezed the trigger once. The retort of the shot was a snapping punch of sound that split the night for an instant. I fired as I ran. I fired with my arm swaying, and my hand trembling, and in hindsight, I was lucky I didn't shoot Harrigan accidentally.

The zombie lunged from behind Harrigan and to his left. My shot went wide. I heard the sound of breaking glass and figured I had probably just killed a window. I fired again and missed again. Harrigan glared at me in horrified alarm.

"Behind you!" I gasped. My breath sawed in my throat.

The zombie lunged. It was like a scene from a horror film; a huge hulking ethereal shape appearing from out of the darkened grey mist of the storm, snarling with rage at an innocent man's unprotected back.

There was nothing more I could do except run. I didn't dare fire again.

I saw the instant my words registered. I saw the flash of recognition and alarm in Harrigan's eyes. I saw him turn, spinning on his heel in the slick muddy grass, and the menacing shape of the crow-bar suddenly seem to become an extension of his arm. He spun like a dancer; incredibly lithe for such a big man, hunching instinctively as he pirouetted, so that the zombie lunged at the place he had been standing just an instant before. It clawed into empty air, and Harrigan rose to full height again in one fluid move, thrusting up from his legs and using his momentum and his bulk to swing all of his weight behind the arc of the crow-bar.

The sound was dreadful – something I will never forget. It was the sickening sound of bone shattering, and the meaty slap as the heavy metal crow-bar claw buried itself into the zombie's spine. The ghoul cried out but did not fall. It was thrown forward by the force of the blow. It took three staggering steps and the crow-bar was torn from Harrigan's hand. Then the ghoul turned and hissed at Harrigan. The big man flinched. The ghoul lunged for him again. Harrigan swayed his head aside, like a boxer ducking inside a jab, and then he lost his footing in the grass and fell backwards into the mud.

By then Jed and I were across the street. Jed snapped his wrist and his Glock seemed to appear miraculously in his hand. Jed didn't wait. He fired a shot from just a few feet that tore into the ghoul's chest and sent it staggering backwards on the lawn. The sound of the bullet seemed to echo off the low clouds. Jed fired again, this time taking a hundredth of a second to aim. I saw the bullet tear into the ghoul's heart, and Jed's arm flung high by the recoil of the weapon. The zombie spun in a tight circle, its arms flailing like it was on fire – but it didn't go down. I stared on in rising terror. The ghoul turned on Jed and lunged towards him.

Jed fired a third shot from so close that the muzzle-flash of the weapon seemed to reach out and touch the undead. The bullet smashed through the zombie's eye socket and splattered us with flesh and thick ooze. The ghoul was flung backwards, falling into the long grass.

It didn't move again.

Jed stood over the body. He was breathing raggedly. I saw him wipe the rain from his eyes and scrape his hands down the side of his face. His fingers were trembling. He stared at me for long seconds of disbelief, and I stared back. Then he took an almighty swing with his leg and kicked the heavy shape in the ribs. The corpse was rolled onto its side, and Jed crouched down in the grass and retrieved the crow-bar.

I went to Harrigan and hauled him to his feet. He was gasping for breath. We all were.

"It kept coming," Harrigan said incredulously. "Wouldn't go down. I buried the crow-bar in the monster's back, and it just hissed at me..."

I nodded, but I was impatient. I grabbed Harrigan's arm and dug my fingers into his flesh. "Clinton, we haven't got time for this right now," I said urgently. "Later. Right now we need to get to that helicopter."

He nodded dazedly and his eyes were glazed and vacant, like he was replaying the moment in his mind. Jed handed me the crow-bar and I shoved it hard at Harrigan.

"Take it," I said, putting an edge on my voice. "And swing it at the next one we see… only be sure to bury the claw in its head. Okay?"

Harrigan nodded. He squeezed his eyes shut tight, and when he opened them again, he seemed clearer – more focused. "Good man. Now move your ass." I slapped him on the back and then turned on my heel and struck out towards the house.

Maybe ten or fifteen seconds had passed from the moment Harrigan had burst from the tree-line and dashed across the road into the path of the undead ghoul. But even ten seconds is a long time when you're standing in the driving rain on a dark and dangerous night. I felt exposed and vulnerable. I had no doubt there were other undead nearby – maybe even in the house we were approaching. I wanted to get into cover. I wanted to be concealed and to make use of terrain and noise of the storm to hide us. Standing on the front lawn of a suburban home was certainly not the best place to hold a committee meeting.

I went forward in a crouch and made my way towards a row of ferns. Once behind their dark bulky shelter, I took a few seconds to study the house.

It was a brick home, built a couple of feet off the ground, with a porch that ran right across the front. I saw the front door. It was open – a dark yawning hole in the façade. Maybe there were more undead waiting inside. Or maybe they had already left the house and were moving in exactly the same direction we were – drawn inexorably towards the screaming flailing sound of the dying helicopter.

I went on grimly, with the Glock thrust out ahead of me, and my eyes swiveling from side to side, all of my senses alert for the slightest sound of danger, or the slightest suggestion of movement. I was soaked to the bone, and my jacket and the nylon bag felt like lead weights.

I reached the back corner of the house and waited without turning. There was dark flat space ahead of us, and then the black border of a fence. Beyond the fence, hanging low in the sky and whipping the air around us into a maddened frenzy, was the helicopter.

"Come on!" I barked, and then sprang instantly to my feet and dashed across the back yard towards the fence. I snagged my shin on something and fell. I immediately leaped to my feet and fixed my eyes on the silhouette of the helicopter. I started running again, then tripped on another solid obstacle and went tumbling face-first back into the wet long grass. Cursing, bruised and a little dazed, I got to my haunches and shook my head. My ears were ringing. I blinked my eyes and peered into the darkness. I couldn't see Jed or Harrigan. I couldn't even sense their presence nearby. I frowned and cursed again. I was near the fence – I could tell that because the whoosh of wind from the helicopter's downdraught was muted, even though the sound was a roaring assault on my ears. I felt my shin through the sodden wet fabric of my jeans. I had no way of knowing if I was bleeding or not, but it hurt. I got slowly to my feet and stared hard into the night.

I stood perfectly still, kept my eyes fixed on the black brooding shape of the house, and waited. I waited to sense some movement – some flicker to my left or right that might suggest Jed or Harrigan were nearby.

Nothing.

I had lost them in the night.

I cursed with bitter frustration – and then I started to sense my own panic begin to rise. I hadn't lost them. They had lost me. I was the one that was alone and on my own. I felt the fear that came with the realization, and I had to crush down on the impulsive urge to scream out, or to reach for the cigarette lighter.

If I had shouted at the top of my lungs, they could not have possibly heard me. The tremendous roar from the helicopter would drown out the sound of explosives. And the lighter was no good. Even in the sheltered lee of the fence, the draught of air being hurled out by the chopper's rotors would make it impossible to get a light. So I stood there – feeling my panic rise, feeling the storm and the rain seem to build towards some ominous crescendo – and I waited, with my nerves fraying until I was on the verge of terror.

Then the night was ripped open by a long jagged bolt of lightning, and a heavy bass rumble of thunder rolled across the clouds and seemed to make the air quiver and the ground beneath my feet tremble. And then a second brilliant jag of lightning ripped the night apart.

In the instant flash of that moment I saw everything.

Harrigan and Jed were still crouched by the corner of the house, and between us, spread across the long green lawn of the back yard, were the dark shapes of at least a dozen dead bodies. They were misshapen mounds, their limbs twisted at impossible angles, their corpses torn and dismembered. They were young and old. They were terribly mutilated.

They were the reason I had tripped and fallen.

I had stumbled over the dead.

I stared aghast – and then, mercifully, the night slammed down like an anvil and the back yard became dark once more.

But the image of that instant was burned into my mind and it stayed with me for long seconds afterwards as my panic returned, multiplied many times over.

Were they dead? I mean *really* dead.

Or were they undead?

Was I standing in a macabre slaughter-yard… or was I about to be set upon by the bodies in the grass, as they rose up from the ground in demented madness and tore me to pieces?

Fear paralyzed me – turned my limbs to lead. I shrank down against the fence and for long seconds I could do nothing more than concentrate on breathing. I closed my eyes and the image of the bodies littered across the lawn came back to me in gory detail. I saw the horror of their pale faces, their bloodied, muddied torsos and the gnawed, severed limbs – and it was so vivid and so confronting that I started to shake. I tore my eyes open, expecting the night to be filled with black hunting shadows – but there was just the howl of the wind and the drumming hiss of the rain. I drew a deep breath and forced myself into action. I fumbled the cigarette lighter from my pocket and flicked it.

The lighter sparked, then was immediately extinguished by the swirling downdrafts of wind. I did it again. And again.

Half a dozen times I flicked the lighter, sending an intermittent pattern of split-second sparks like a marker beacon. Then I leaned back against the fence, and waited – either for the mutilated bodies to rise, or for Jed and Harrigan to find me.

It was impossible to see anything in the crushing dark of the night. Down low against the fence, the ambient orange glow from the distant fires was blocked out, so that all of my senses were heightened – and all of them were utterly useless. My sense of smell was overwhelmed by the thick cloying stench of rotting corpses, and the smell of muddy earth and grass.

I waited.

The trembling in my hands became worse. I was shaking like a leaf. I told myself it was the soaking cold – and maybe it was. Maybe.

My teeth began to chatter and I was overcome by the sudden urge to run – to run anywhere. Just to flee like a coward. I wanted to be away from this place. I wanted to be away from the fear. I wanted to be safe – and I wanted to see again.

More than anything else, I wanted that. The crushing dark and the horror-fueled images in my mind sent my imagination into overdrive. The clatter of the helicopter became the menacing scream of a horde of zombies. The slap of the wind against my neck became the fetid gasping breath of the undead. Alone in the dark, I felt myself unraveling.

I heard it too late – the splashing sound beside me of heavy footsteps. Then I saw movement – just the flicker of a darker shadow, but by the time I saw it, it was too late to react. I had time for a final gasping choking breath – and then whatever moved in the night was upon me.

"Fucker!"

It was Jed. I felt him crash into me and then slump down against the fence, the heat of his body hard against my shoulder. He was panting, his breath sawing raggedly across his throat. Not a second later, the shape of Clinton Harrigan appeared as a drifting black shadow a little to my left. I choked down a cry of panic that was rising up into my throat, and was overwhelmed by a surge of relief. They had found me.

"Fucker!" Jed said again, snarling. He was angry, but it was anger mixed with his own fear, and it flamed as he fumed in outrage.

"You just took off into the dark, you son-of-a-bitch!" Jed hissed. "You just left us."

I shook my head – then realized that in the darkness, shaking my head was a useless gesture. "I didn't leave you," I said. "I just moved before I had time to change my mind. I thought you two were right behind me."

47

I heard Harrigan's voice, sharp and tense, loom out of the night. "Well we weren't," he said. "You should have waited, Mitch. That was stupid. Next time, wait until we're ready. And make sure we know what you're doing. I don't want to go through that again," he said, and there was an ominous tone of warning and suppressed violence in his words that left me in no doubt that he too had been frightened, and that I should not take Harrigan's Christian nature of benign benevolence for granted. He was letting me know that he was a nice guy – because he chose to be.

A warning.

I got to my feet, and groped like a blind man in the dark until I felt Harrigan's shoulder. "Sorry," I said. "I gave us all a fright. It won't happen again."

Harrigan might have said something – I'm not sure, but if he did, his words were drowned out by the sharp sound of Jed suddenly crying out in horror. He was standing on the other side of me. I felt the rub of his shoulder and his rigid tension. "Jesus Christ! Look at that!"

My head snapped round, and I peered over the top of the fence.

My body went ice cold.

I had to screw my eyes into narrow slits against the maniacal shriek of the beaten wind, but that didn't diminish the horror.

The land beyond the fence was clear. It might have been a suburban park, but the grass was long and swaying in the night. It stretched for maybe two hundred yards, and then the ground began to rise gradually to a hilly crest that was built out by suburban homes.

The hill was on fire.

I could see at least a dozen buildings ablaze, the flames flickering into the night sky, as if lashing out in anger at the rain. I couldn't see smoke, but I could smell it in the air, and the burning skyline created a red-orange backlight that gave me a view clear across to the far side of the park.

In the night sky – not fifty feet from the fence – was the dark shape of the helicopter. It was very low, the skids beneath the fuselage seeming to scrape and slash at the grass as the craft swayed perilously from side to side. But even so close, and even with the fire blazing across the distant hills, still the helicopter's shape was dull and blurred, and I realized it was because the helicopter had been painted black.

I felt Harrigan suddenly squeeze my arm, and his grip was vice-like and painful.

"We've got problems," he said.

I frowned, not understanding – and then saw a blur of movement in the distance.

I stared for long seconds. The rain was a grey misting curtain that beat down in a vertical haze. But through it – right on the edge of the field, I suddenly saw several shapes. They moved like ghostly apparitions, seeming to hover and undulate through the driving squalls. The shapes were lit by the glow of the fire, but it was an uncertain light, and it took me many moments before I suddenly realized what I was seeing.

There was at least a dozen of them – a dozen undead – drifting through the long grass of the field, drawn towards the sound of the helicopter, and moving in a long ragged line, like a pack of wolves stalking a wounded prey.

I heard movement in the dark beside me and I glanced sideways. It was Jed, his big muscled frame hanging against the fence and peering into the night – seeing the horror that I was seeing, and, by the sound of his voice, feeling the same fear.

"We can't fight them all off."

"I know," I agreed. "Not with a couple of pistols and a crow-bar."

I tore my eyes back to the bucking, swaying shape of the helicopter. "If he doesn't try to land now, they'll be on him before we can rescue him."

My attention snapped back to the approaching shapes of the undead. They were like flickering mirages, moving quickly through the dark. I tried to calculate the angles and get a sense of how close the undead were – and how much time the pilot had before they would be upon him – and us.

It wasn't long. Maybe sixty seconds. If the pilot didn't set the helicopter down right now, it would be too late – for all of us.

At that moment a building on the crest of the distant hill seemed to explode in a huge column of flame, and in the flare of brighter light, the line of zombies suddenly took on sharp outline and solid form. Behind them, other dull drifting shapes were beginning to loom out of the night.

"There's more of them," I said ominously. They were filling the dark streets, spilling from the nearest houses. A road ran parallel to the far side of the park, and I could see burned out vehicles and dark shapes laying on the blacktop like small broken toys as the undead gathered into a milling, swaying tide that began to uncoil and surge down into the long grass of the field behind the first line of hunters.

"What are we going to do?" Jed asked.

I didn't answer for a long moment. The line of zombies on the edge of the field seemed to stop moving closer, but I knew it was just a trick of the poor light. They would still be moving – still stalking their way forward. I glanced up at the helicopter again, and as I did it seemed to swing directly overhead, and then tilt at an obscene angle. It veered back over the long grass of the field, but it was lower now. The shaft of the spotlight suddenly blinked on, and the patch of ground beneath the hull was turned bright as daylight. It lasted for only a few seconds – long enough to give the pilot a chance to sight the ground, and long enough to completely destroy my night vision.

I turned my head away – but the flare of the light was burned onto my eyes. When I opened them again and looked back across the field, the wavering line of undead was blurred and indistinct.

"We've got no choice," I said with a sense of rising fear and anxiety. "We have to rescue that pilot – if he survives the landing. There's no other option. We're dead men if we don't."

The helicopter tilted up on its tail rotor like a rearing horse, and hung in mid air for a moment, its nose pointing towards the clouds.

Then it just stopped flying.

Stopped – and fell out of the sky.

The big whining engine died – and for an instant the night was perfectly silent.

But just for an instant.

Then the helicopter dropped like a stone. The heavy weight of the nose fell towards the ground, but the helicopter was not high enough in the sky for the front-end to gather momentum, and so the craft dropped in a flat fall – the skids collapsed and the dead-weight of the machine crumpled the hull in a shattering collision that shook the ground beneath my feet. Grass and mud were hurled into the sky. The rotor blades flailed, and then tore off. Grinding, tearing metal shredded through the air as the machine ripped itself to pieces, and the sky was filled with a thousand flying shards of splintered death.

"Oh my God," I heard Clinton Harrigan breathe, and for long seconds we could do nothing more than stare, numb and dazed and appalled, until the dust cleared and the sound of the collision faded.

At last, the night was silent.

At last, the helicopter was down.

But the danger was only just beginning.

Chapter Two.

"Come on!" Harrigan cried, and we went at the fence in a rain-soaked awkward tangle of knees and elbows.

I went over in the long soft grass, feeling the weight of the nylon bag's contents pushing me down like extra gravity, and I sank in the soft muddy earth to my ankles.

The fiery glow of the distant burning buildings gave good light and we ran towards the crumpled wreck of the helicopter with no thought of stealth. It was a race against time.

Jed pulled ahead of me – he was big and fit and strong, and I kept my eyes on the broad of his back as he ran with his legs high through the grass, like a man running into beachside surf. He reached the nose of the helicopter and I saw him crouch there, peering past broken twisted metal, while Harrigan and I struggled to catch up.

I ran with my eyes moving everywhere, trying to take in everything in an instant. The undead were much closer now – they were solid shambling shapes that were sweeping towards us like a dark ragged tide. The helicopter was badly damaged. The whole underbelly of the craft seemed to have split wide open. The tail section had broken off: it lay in the grass like a dismembered limb, and as I got closer, the ground became a series of deep troughs and furrows where the rotors had cleaved gouts out of the soft earth before splintering and breaking. I could see the cockpit door. It was hanging open – as if the lock had been sprung by the shattering impact as the helicopter crashed to the ground.

I ran faster. Harrigan was at my shoulder. I was breathing hard from the effort, my nerves screwed up tight.

I saw Jed turn his head towards the approaching zombies, and then quickly back to us. He had the Glock in his hand, resting it on a piece of the broken helicopter.

"Check the pilot," he said urgently as we got nearer. "I'll keep an eye on the bastards. When I start shooting, you'll know it's time to get the hell out of here."

"Okay," I gasped. It was all I had breath for. I felt the strain of fatigue in my shoulders and legs, and my lungs were burning from the effort. I went straight for the cockpit door. Jed turned back towards the zombie tide.

The door was crumpled, and hanging at an angle off one broken hinge – but for all that, it was stuck. I hooked my hand inside the door and heaved. The door moved an inch or two – just far enough for me to see inside the dark cockpit. I could see the shape of the pilot. He was hunched against the straps of his safety harness, his head slumped forward, his arms limp at his side. He wasn't moving.

"Clinton!" I shouted. The big man was close beside me. There was a sliding door behind the cockpit. It was buckled and folded into the wrecked fuselage. He turned to me, and his eyes were wide and panicked. "Give me the crow-bar."

I braced the bar against the door and heaved. The sound of rending, tearing metal was suddenly loud in the night. The door moved a couple of inches. Harrigan elbowed me out of the way impatiently and hefted the bar. "Let me."

I stood back, hands on my knees, and sucked in deep breaths. My lungs felt like they were on fire.

I heard Harrigan grunt and saw the strain contort his face as he put all of his weight against the door. It held for another long moment – and then groaned open, buckling in the center, as the thin metal peeled apart like opening a can.

He threw down the crow-bar and wrapped his big hands around the door. It came all the way open in a final tear of metal and smashed back against the broken side of the machine.

I dived into the cockpit. The air was filled with the smell of gasoline and smoke. The control panel had been driven against the pilot's legs and lower body by the impact of the collision. I glanced through the crazed, shattered Plexiglas of the cockpit bubble. There were splashes of blood against the screen – and through it, I saw the nearest undead ghouls, approaching fast. I tore my eyes away and turned my attention back to the pilot.

He was wearing headphones. I snatched them off, and when I did, the man's head rolled heavily to the side. I felt under his jaw for a pulse, but my hands were shaking and my breath sawing so loudly, I couldn't feel or hear anything. I slapped my hand hard against his chest and it came away wet and sticky.

Blood. Oozing from a small hole in the man's chest. I couldn't see a lot in the gloomy darkness, but I used up a few precious seconds to explore

55

the wound with my fingers before quickly moving on.

It took me a moment to find the release locks on the pilot's safety harness. The broken console of lights and gauges had been driven into his lap. I thumped the releases and the straps went loose. The man's body slumped sideways against the far door of the cockpit. He didn't move.

I turned back to Harrigan. The big man's face was framed in the wrecked opening. "He's dead," I said. "Dammit."

Harrigan seemed to deflate, like the last flickering light of hope had just been extinguished. He sagged against the side of the helicopter. I began to back quickly out of the cockpit. It was a cramped, tangled tomb and I was terrified by the smell of fuel. The helicopter was like a ticking time bomb.

I got half-way out, my eyes fixed on the approaching undead, when I noticed a sudden movement in the corner of my eye. My head snapped round. Trapped behind the pilot's seat within the fuselage of the crumpled machine were two other people.

A man and a girl.

The man was moving – moving his hand. It flopped on his lap in small desperate movements like a landed fish.

"Jesus!" I swore. And then I started to shout. "Are you okay? Can you hear me?"

I didn't wait for any long-winded answers. The man's hand flicked again, and I saw the girl beside him roll her head so that it slumped heavily to rest against the man's shoulder. I backed out of the cockpit and shoved my face close to Harrigan's.

"There's two people in there – alive," I said tensely.

Harrigan's eyes widened in relief and shock. "Are you for real?"

I nodded my head. "They're in the cabin. We've got to get the back door open."

He grabbed my arm to stop me as I lunged for the sliding door. "Let me do it."

Harrigan attacked the door with the crow-bar, but when the helicopter had crashed, the closest side of the machine had taken the brunt of initial impact. The metal of the door had folded and creased within the frame of the dead machine, so that it was impossible to force it open. Harrigan looked at me heavily, and shook his head. "It won't budge. I'm going to have to try the other side."

I felt an instant surge of alarm. I looked up, past the sheltering shape of the helicopter and the zombies were now much nearer. Maybe fifty paces. I could see them as clear figures; undead men and women moving hungrily closer through the grass, haloed by the red glow of the distant burning buildings on the hillside.

I looked back at Harrigan and nodded. "I'll come with you. Be quick about it."

We skirted the broken tail section of the helicopter and ran around to the far side of the fuselage. I felt completely exposed – like hapless prey. Harrigan attacked the door with every last ounce of his remaining energy – and I went down on one knee and carefully aimed the Glock at the closest undead.

It was a man. He seemed taller than the others in the line. He was wearing some kind of a jacket. It seemed to hang off his lanky frame. His movements were jerky – as though his undead body was overcome by repeated convulsions. His head swayed from side to side and his arm and leg movements were awkward ungainly jerks, so that he looked like some kind of mechanical robot with bad wiring.

I aimed the pistol at the man's head, remembering our earlier near-death encounter on the footpath. The gun felt heavy in my hands, and I could feel strain and tension in my shoulders, and all the way down to my wrist. I held the weapon steady, took a long deep breath – and waited.

Behind me Clinton Harrigan was using words that Christians would never find in the Bible, of that I am sure. He cursed vehemently and I heard the clang of the crow-bar as he attacked the cabin door with the desperation of a man about to die. I heard a high-pitched squeal of metal against metal that set my teeth on edge.

"How are you going?" I shouted over my shoulder at Harrigan without taking my eyes off the figure of the tall zombie approaching. I tried to keep my voice calm, but I had to shout over the sound of the drumming rain, and the God-awful thump that was my pounding, racing heart. My voice came out, sounding unnaturally loud in my ears, like a desperate squeak.

Harrigan said nothing. I heard him grunt, and then he cursed again. I heard the crow-bar clang off metal.

I felt like I was kneeling under a spotlight. There was no shelter on this side of the helicopter – no shadow to hide in. Harrigan and I were totally exposed by the glow of the distant fires. I stole a glance sideways to where Jed had taken position at the nose of the helicopter, but I couldn't see him.

A sudden sense of isolation swept over me. I should have been able to see Jed. He had propped his gun arm on a piece of wreckage near the crumpled front-end of the helicopter. I felt a sudden sense of unease.

"Jed...?"

Nothing. No answer.

I called again, this time more urgently. "Jed."

There was another long moment of silence. I flicked my eyes back anxiously to the line of undead. They were just thirty yards away.

"Jed!"

I heard a scuffle of movement, and then my brother's voice, tense and harsh from somewhere behind me. "Shut up, jerk weed, and get ready to drop the fuckers!"

I heard Harrigan groan and strain, like the sound a man makes when he lifts a great weight. The sound went on for long seconds – and then I heard a mighty slam of metal. Harrigan gave a ragged shout of triumph, and I couldn't help myself – I turned back to stare at the helicopter.

Harrigan was slumped against the broken fuselage of the craft, his chest heaving like a bellows, his face turned up into the rain and the storm, his eyes screwed tightly shut as though racked with some great pain.

Beside him, the cabin door was open – a dark space that held our last hope of survival.

I stuffed the Glock down the waistband of my jeans and turned back to the open cabin door. It was gloomy inside. The man was slumped against the mangled internal frame of the hull, leaning heavily against the safety strap of his safety belt. Beside him, was a teenage girl. She had dark hair. Her eyes were closed and her face was white as marble.

I glanced at the man's face. He was about my age – maybe a few years closer to forty. He was a big, broad-shouldered man wearing a dark suit. His face was wide, his features unremarkable. He had a buzz-cut hairstyle, shaved very short so that my first impression was that he could easily be military. He had that look about him. I reached for his face and cupped my hand under his jaw to feel for a pulse. As I did, the man's eyes flicked open, bright and clear and sharp. He blinked at me – and then made a slow, low groaning sound. His hand came from his lap to feel for a bump I saw on his forehead that was the size of a golf ball. I gently trapped his hand and eased it back to his side.

"You're okay," I said with conviction I did not feel. I wasn't a doctor. I had no medical training at all – but it seemed like the right thing to say, and I doubted there was any point in telling the man otherwise. It wasn't going to make any difference...

He stared at me for long seconds, his expression blank, but I sensed there was plenty going on behind his dark eyes. The lump on his head was swelling and turning dark red. I thumped the release catch on his safety belt.

"Do you think you can move?"

The man nodded – and then winced painfully. He turned his head very slowly, as though it were some fragile precious thing made of delicate glass. "Check Millie," the man said. His voice was croaky. He licked his lips, and then said in an unnaturally loud voice, "she's my daughter."

I nodded. The man leaned himself aside and I reached across him. As the man adjusted his position, the girl's head rolled from his shoulder, and I caught her cheek in the palm of my hand. Her skin was smooth, her face warm. I eased her head back against the padding of the seat and felt for a pulse: faint and racing, fluttering under the soft flesh of her jawline.

"She's alive," I declared. "But I need you out of here so I can help her. Understand?"

The man nodded again – this time very carefully. I heaved myself back out of the mangled wreckage and the man reached for my shoulder to support his weight. He groaned painfully, and I felt his big fingers dig into the muscles of my forearm. I reached out with my free hand to help him and he came out of the helicopter into the pouring rain on shaky, unsteady legs.

I left him.

I leaned back into the helicopter and perched myself awkwardly on the narrow bench seat beside the girl. I was soaking wet. Rain dripped from my hair and my face, and my fingers were stiff and trembling from the cold. She was dressed in jeans and a dark sweater. I reached for the girl's arms and moved them slowly and carefully. Then I ran my hands all the way down to her wrists, feeling for anything that might be broken. She was wearing some kind of a chunky, decorative bracelet. I saw her eyelids flutter. I reached for her legs and felt from her ankle to her knee, squeezing each one gently and watching the girl's face for a reaction.

Nothing.

In hindsight, I was probably doing all the things that would have given any medical man worth his salt convulsions of alarm, but I simply didn't know what else to do. From my rudimentary inspection, the girl seemed to have no obvious broken bones – and that was a good thing.

I felt the back of her neck, and then ran my fingers lightly across her forehead and temple. I could feel no bumps, and sensed no bleeding. I slid the heavy bracelet up her arm a little and checked the pulse at her wrist. It was still erratic – and then I heard a gunshot.

My head snapped round and I stared out through the opening of the cabin. The man and Harrigan were standing in the way so I couldn't see much past their big frames. I sensed the line of undead was gathering itself like a mighty wave that curls over bathers at the instant before it breaks, and pounds them under the crushing impact.

I turned back – and got the shock of my life. The girl's eyes were open and she was staring at me. Staring at me like I was some fascinating specimen at a zoo. Her eyes were enormous dark, dazed pools, set against the drawn pale complexion of her face. Her lips moved – she opened her mouth and exhaled a ragged uncertain breath.

"Who are you?" she asked. Her voice was barely more than a whisper, inflected with neither fear or alarm – merely idle curiosity, as though she had just woken from a deep sleep and enquired about the weather.

"I'm Mitch," I said gently. "I'm here to help you."

I sensed the doorway behind me darkening, and I glanced over my shoulder. The man was standing there, blocking out the fiery glow of the night, his suit already soaked and clinging to the silhouette of his muscled frame.

"Millie's my daughter," the man said – and again I noticed how unnaturally loud his voice was, and how pointed his tone. I wondered absently if he had suffered damage to his hearing in the crash and that perhaps the sounds around him were somehow muted so that he felt forced to speak so loudly – like someone singing with headphones always sings louder than they realize. But I had no time then to ponder the problem. I leaned over the girl and gently wrapped my arm around her shoulder. "We have to get you out of here," I said, and then, like a fool, I added, "there are undead zombies close by, and there is a fuel leak. The helicopter might explode at any moment."

I regretted my words instantly. The girl went from dazed and relaxed and compliant, to near hysterical with fear. She threw herself at me, flailing arms and hands and knees in a desperate attempt to get out of the helicopter. I tried to help, but the girl was suddenly near-crazed. I backed out of the helicopter and the girl came at me like a caged lion.

No broken bones – that was for sure.

We stood in a tight knot beside the helicopter. The man went to the girl and wrapped a protective arm around her shoulder. She leaned into him – not overcome with affection, but rather like someone who takes shelter behind a large boulder. It was instinctive. Then I saw the man snap to full alertness. "My gun!" he said.

I stared at him. "Where is it?"

He was padding down his pockets, becoming frantic. Maybe he was from the military, or maybe ex-military. For guys who have served, I guessed their weapon was an extension of their body. "It must still be in the helicopter," he said – and scrambled head-first back through the dark opening.

I turned back to the line of undead. I saw Jed now. He was *inside* the broken cockpit of the helicopter, firing through the shattered Plexiglas. He was concealed behind the dead body of the pilot, aiming carefully at the dark looming shapes of death.

I heard the roar of his Glock, tearing through the hissing sound of the rain, and then snapped my eyes to the line of undead. I saw one of them suddenly double over and clutch at its stomach. It was a woman – I think. The figure had long straggly hair and was thinly built. It was about fifteen yards away. It froze for a split-second, and then slowly toppled backwards into the grass. I heard Jed give a ragged cheer. "I got one!" – then the sound was cut off by another rumble of thunder that boomed overhead.

And then a remarkable thing happened. The line of undead stopped. Froze. They were close enough to see physical details now – close enough to hear the sound of them shambling towards us in the long grass as the noise of the rain ebbed and flowed. I sensed the hunched, prowling way they held themselves, like mad dogs that drop their heads and bunch their shoulders when on the scent of prey.

For a second nothing at all happened. I saw undead heads turn towards the place in the line where the woman ghoul had fallen. Then I saw the attitude of the others seem to change. I heard one of the ghouls growl – and it was a chilling, terrible sound, quickly imitated by others. The cry went up – and then the zombies nearest the woman lunged towards the place where she had fallen. They were snarling and roaring – gnashing teeth and clawing. I saw one of the undead rise up, and he had a forearm in his bloodied hands, gnawing at it with rabid madness.

I heard fabric tearing, and then the horrific sound of bones cracking and flesh ripping. Another of the ghouls reeled away into the darkness and his hands were full and heavy with dripping bloodied organs that slithered in his fingers like tentacles.

I heard Clinton Harrigan's voice behind me, and his words were numbed and slowed by incredulous horror.

"Holy Mary, mother of God..."

And then a louder, more urgent voice that could only be my brother's, shouting the words that my brain was shouting at the same instant.

"Run! Now!"

I didn't turn away from the horror. The ghouls were in a frenzy, dismembering the corpse in the grass. I saw only hunched shoulders and flailing arms beating the grass into maddened swishing tails, but I could imagine the gory detail. Snap-shot images of the slaughter-yard scene in the backyard came back to haunt me.

Jed fired again. And again.

I drew the Glock from my jeans and fired into the dark mass of bodies. I don't know if I hit anything – I just fired. Then I fired again. I heard a sudden new sound – the sound of different gunfire, the noise of it slamming in my ears – and without turning I guessed the man had recovered his weapon from where it had fallen.

I sensed that Jed's words had culminated into panicked action behind me. I heard heavy footsteps, pounding in the sloshing mud, and when I glanced over my shoulder, I was alone. Harrigan, the man and the girl had disappeared round behind the darkened, shadowed shelter of the broken helicopter. I wanted to run after them. Cowardice and regret compounded. I wasn't made of the right stuff for a heroic last stand. I wanted to run too.

I fired twice more. The gun leaped in my hand and I saw one of the dark savage shapes roll away from the milling gnashing pack.

"Jed?"

I knew he was still nearby. I had heard one of his shots rip the night apart, just a moment after I had fired. His voice came back to me, clear and close.

"Yeah?"

"It's time to go," I said. "Where are the others?"

There was a pause, and in that moment of silence I shuffled backwards until I felt the frame of the helicopter press against my legs.

"They're going back over the fence," I heard Jed say. He was moving as he spoke, coming closer. Then I saw him round the nose of the helicopter and stride towards me. The ground was a quagmire of rutted muddy troughs from where the helicopter's crash landing had torn the earth to pieces.

Other undead shapes were filling the skyline, sweeping down from the hillside streets and coming across the field. And I saw more dark movement to our left – just flickering shadows that might have been wind-tossed branches – but might also have been more undead hunting their way towards us from surrounding houses. I'd had enough. My nerves were frayed.

"Let's get out of here," I said urgently. "It's time for a cowardly retreat. We've done enough. Time to save our asses."

I glanced at Jed. The bastard was smiling – not because I was funny, but because he was enjoying himself. I could see it in the glint of his eyes. There was a macabre sense of joy for him in shooting and killing, and I had to grab his arm and push him away into the darkness, even as he continued to fire.

We slipped back into the dark cover of the shadows and I ran like the hounds of Hell were on my heels. In fact, they probably were. Once the undead body Jed had shot had been torn to pieces, they would want more prey. They seemed possessed by some insane killing frenzy and blood-lust that had shocked and appalled me. I didn't want to be the next victim.

I heard Jed at my shoulder, his long legs taking big splashing strides. We hit the fence at a run, and he went over like a pole-vaulter, while I slammed into the palings and clambered with frantic, frenzied fingers until I could heave myself over and drop down into the relative safety of the darkened back yard.

Out of the frying pan…

I dropped down into the darkness, remembering the dismembered bodies, and the images of slaughter that I had seen just minutes earlier. I called out to Jed in a strained whisper and waited in the eerie heavy silence for a reply.

"I'm right here," Jed answered from very close by. His voice was gravel-like. "Next to you."

I hesitated for a moment. I couldn't see him. "What are you doing?"

Another long pause, and when he answered, his tone was somehow obscene.

"I'm watching them."

"What?"

"I'm watching them," he said with fascination. "They're at the helicopter."

"Are... are they coming this way?"

"They're coming from everywhere."

"This way?" I felt my strained nerves rise again in alarm.

"No." He might have shaken his head. I couldn't tell.

"What are they doing?"

"The pilot," Jed said in awe. "They're tearing the body to pieces. I've never seen anything like it."

I didn't know what to say – so I said nothing. I crouched there, against the fence, and after another moment I felt Jed crouch down beside me so I could feel his knee against mine. He was breathing hard.

I figured Harrigan would have taken the man and the girl no further than the corner of the house. That meant weaving our way through the tangle of dismembered bodies. For no good reason I glanced up at the sky. It was still raining, and the night was blanketed by the dark scudding shape of clouds being shredded by the wind. I caught a brief glimpse of the moon and then it was swallowed once more by the night.

I dug the lighter from my pocket and hunched down low against the fence. I cupped my hand close, and the lighter flamed into a tiny golden glow. Jed's face looked dark and haunted, his eyes sunken shadows against the swollen shape of his cheek and the peak of his nose. His expression was grim.

"Keep your hand on my shoulder. I'll lead you," I said. "We're making for the corner of the house where you and Harrigan got left. That's where I think the others will be waiting."

Jed nodded. The flicker of light didn't last – nor did I expect it to. As soon as we stood, the wind extinguished the little flame. But it had burned long enough, and I hoped that Harrigan was waiting at the edge of the house. If he were, he would have seen the flame. He would know we were coming towards him.

I went with all the hasty caution I could muster – shuffling my feet like a blind man in a minefield, and going as quickly as I dared. Twice I felt my toe scuff against something soft and unnatural – and each time I veered a few paces to the side to avoid whatever lay there.

It seemed to take forever – but it was maybe a minute or two, before we saw the heavy dark shadow of the side of the house – a shade darker than the night itself. I heard Harrigan clear his throat, and went towards the sound.

He was there. They all were – crouched on the narrow pathway that we had taken from the road. I dropped to my knees and we all huddled for a moment without saying anything – but merely feeling the strength and comfort that comes from not being alone – not being isolated.

Finally I heard the man's voice. He was whispering, and there was a strained edge in his tone. I sensed he was somewhere close to my left, and I figured his daughter would be beside him.

"No noise from now on," he said, sounding like he knew what he was talking about. "They hear everything," he said. Harrigan took a deep breath and held it. I think I did too. "Is anyone injured?"

No one said anything.

"Good," the man said. "They're attracted to blood."

"Are you sure?" It was Jed's voice, curious, not concerned.

"I'm sure," the man said – and once again I sensed he was speaking from some knowledge or experience.

"Okay," I muttered, feeling instantly self-conscious for speaking after we had just agreed to make no noise – but this had to be said. "We're not going back to the house – there's no point. And we can't stay here, in this house. It's too damned close, and the yard is full of dead bodies, so God knows what it's like inside."

"So what's the plan?" That was Harrigan. His voice sounded like he was across the huddle from me.

"We go sideways," I said. "This is a long street. So we move a few houses along. Maybe half a dozen – enough to be away from the helicopter and away from the field. Hopefully that will be far enough. We'll find a place and hide up for the night."

No one objected, so I got to my feet and moved a few yards back along the pathway towards the front of the house until I found a gap in the line of shrubs and bushes that must have served as a nature fence between the next property. I clambered through with my jaw clenched, wincing

71

at the sound of rustling leaves and twigs, and hoping that the storm would last long enough to mask our escape.

I waited on the other side of the bush until everyone was through and gathered around me. Jed was the last man. Then I led them at a bent-over crouch past the front of the neighboring house, making use of the shadows and moving with slow deliberate steps, gritting my teeth as every new noise we made became an agonizing torture.

The lawns were sodden – the ground turned to mud. Every step was fraught with the danger of a twisted ankle or worse. It took agonizing minutes of strained tension until we had passed four houses, moving at some kind of an angle to the site of the helicopter crash.

The strain was unrelenting. There was not a single moment when I didn't feel like I was one step away from death or danger. By the time we had passed two more houses I was a wreck of nerves to the point where I felt physically ill, and I knew I couldn't go on much further.

I lifted my head. We were crouched in the dark shadow of a huge tree in the corner of a front yard. I could see the outline of an old car tire suspended from a low branch and swinging from the end of a rope. I glanced towards the house, but it was simply too dark to tell anything other than it seemed to be high – maybe two stories. I went towards the shape of the building carefully.

As I got closer, small details began to fill in. It was brick. I could see the dark shape of a window, and then I stumbled into a garden – and walked into the side of a low cement wall. It was as high as my knee. I tried to clamber over it, and then realized it was a verandah. I stepped up into sudden shelter from the wind and the rain – and the abrupt silence was ominous and eerie.

I waited for the others, and as I did I took tentative steps along the porch. It was good to feel solid ground beneath my feet. We had sloshed in mud and grass for so long the muscles in my calves and thighs were burning. A full-length dark rectangle loomed out of the night as a pitch black shape.

"The door has been left wide open," I said in a whisper, and stepped cautiously towards the dark breach.

I smacked my face hard against cold glass.

I had walked into a window – not a door. It felt like I had broken my nose, and my eyes watered.

I heard Jed stifle a snigger.

The front door was a few feet further along.

It was locked.

Jed forced it open.

Chapter Three.

We stood in a small entry area and Harrigan quietly closed the door behind us. We were in a tight phalanx, with Jed and I at the front, Glocks drawn, and the man right behind us, his pistol thrusting out beside Jed. The girl was wedged between Harrigan and the man – and we stood frozen like that for long seconds, expecting and anticipating the night to come alive with dark vicious shapes.

The air was stale and thick with the stench of rotting decomposition. The taste of it painted the back of my throat like a coat of tar.

My hands were shaking – I was shivering from the cold, and trembling from a new surge of nervous adrenalin. I fumbled in my pocket with my free hand and flicked on the cigarette lighter. I had two candles in the nylon bag on my back, but I daren't light them. Not yet.

The lighter threw out a surprisingly bright glow that illuminated the area around us and gave me a chance to get my bearings.

We were in a small living room. There were a couple of recliner sofa chairs arranged around a blank television screen, and there were framed photos hanging on the wall beside us. There was the dark squat shape of an open fireplace in a nearby corner. The rest of the room faded off into dark gloom.

We stood, shivering and trembling, and dripping water onto the carpet for perhaps a minute before I took the first tentative steps into the room. I went sideways – to the full-length window – and dragged the drapes across to shut out the light. The noise was loud in the silence and I felt myself wincing. The cigarette lighter went out. I quickly flicked it back on and turned to study the room proper. On the far side of the room was a narrow hallway, leading deeper into darkness. There were thick rugs on the floor, and a low timber side-table beside one of the chairs. The table was littered with tiny plastic bottles and a scatter of small colored tablets. There were more tablets spilled across the floor.

Sitting in the chair, with her head thrown back against the padded upholstery, and her mouth wide open, was an elderly woman. I took three steps towards the sofa, my shoes sodden and squelching.

The woman was quite dead.

Her eyes were open, sunken deep into the skeleton of her face. Her skin was grey and drawn tight. She had been very old. There was a walking stick on the floor by her feet. She had been dead for quite some time – several days, if not a week or more. Her tongue was thick and swollen in her mouth, and the body had bloated. The stench of rotting meat from the corpse was sickly sweet and nauseating. Her clothes were filthy with her own fluids. I reeled away and turned back to the others.

"Dead woman," I said softly. "Clinton, keep the girl there until I can find something to cover the body."

There was another window in the room and I went to it and drew the curtains tightly together.

Then I unslung the nylon bag and dropped to my haunches. I felt suddenly light – like I was floating on the air. I hadn't realized how heavy the bag had been. I felt a burning ache in my shoulders where the thin straps had rubbed my skin raw, but I ignored the pain and fetched one of the candles from the bag. I lit it and waited until the flame flickered and glowed into life.

The light was tentative and uncertain – but it was better than stumbling around in the dark. The candle flame flared more brightly, and cast soft dark shadows onto the walls. But more than the light, it provided comfort – some primitive instinctive sense, I suppose.

I carried the candle with me and got as far as the opening to the hallway. Then I turned back to where the rest of the group stood waiting.

"Jed. Come with me."

He loomed out of the gloom, swarthy and grim-faced, but there was a strange, pained look in my brother's eyes. I didn't say anything. I simply turned and headed down the passage with him close behind me.

We prowled the hallway, my gun held stiff-armed out in front of me, my whole body twisting left and right from the hips as we crept through the house.

There was a neat little kitchen, a laundry, a bathroom, and a couple of bedrooms. We went through the house drawing every curtain tightly closed.

The first bedroom we found was packed with stored pieces of furniture, all covered with heavy white sheets. I dragged one of the sheets off an antique-looking wardrobe and slung it over my shoulder.

There were two more dead bodies in the second bedroom.

A man and a woman.

They might have been in their forties. It was hard to tell. They were lying in the bed. The woman's face had been shattered by a single gunshot. The bullet had torn up through her jaw and ripped the top of her skull open. Blood, thick clumps of gore, and tufts of blonde hair were spattered across the wall and the bedhead. Blood soaked the sheets.

Beside her was the body of a man. Maybe it was her husband. It looked like he had thrust a gun into his mouth and pulled the trigger. He had fallen sideways, so that his body was lying slumped across the woman's. Both the bodies were bloated with gases, and the air in the room was rancid. I saw a little silver revolver on the bedroom floor, close beside the bed.

While Jed stood in the doorway, I ransacked the wardrobes and bedside chests of drawers for clothes. I dumped them hurriedly at the door to the bathroom and then we took the candle back into the kitchen and searched every cupboard. There were cans of soup, beans, and ham in a pantry, beside a full carton of soda. There were more cans of soda in the refrigerator.

Enough food and drink to last several days.

I sighed my relief, and then carried the dust sheet back through to the living room and covered the old woman. Then Jed and I dragged her body down the hallway and left it lying in the laundry. We pulled the door shut.

I set the first candle on the living room floor, then took the second one from the bag and lit it. I handed it to Jed and he perched it on top of the television set. The flare from the two small flickering flames was enough to cast the entire room in a dim warm glow. Harrigan, the girl and the man peeled away from the darkness of the foyer and slumped with weary exhaustion to the ground.

"There's plenty of food, and plenty to drink in the kitchen," I said softly. "And I've found clothes," I added. "I've left them at the door to the bathroom." I turned to the girl and stared at her. Her long dark hair was plastered flat to her skull in messy tangles, and her face was drawn and very pale. She looked very small and fragile. It was the first time I had taken notice of her. I guessed she was maybe fifteen years old. She had dark, sad eyes. "I don't think anything will fit very well, but at least you will be dry. Take the candle with you and get changed. You can't stay in those wet clothes."

The girl glanced to her father and I saw him nod. Then she got to her feet and took the candle from the television. She took two tentative steps towards the darkness, and then stopped. She turned back.

"Come with me," she said to her father, her voice timid and fearful. "Just to the end of the hall."

The man nodded and got to his feet. He followed the girl, gun drawn, and I watched the tiny soft glow of the candle in her hands fade as she disappeared deeper into the house.

Jed, Harrigan and I sat in absolute silence, staring down into the flame of the candle between us, each of us lost in our own thoughts. It wasn't a numbed, horrified silence – not for me at least. I was contemplative. I'm not a Rhodes scholar, and I don't have a university education – but I'm not a fool. I've learned enough about life to be wary, and how to read subtle signs. Some of the signals I was getting from the man and girl made me suspicious. But not suspicious enough to voice my concerns – not until I'd had the time to ask questions and to get answers.

And I had a lot of questions.

I glanced across at Jed. He was staring back at me with dark eyes. The light from the candle leaped and flickered so that his expression looked wicked and malevolent.

Jed I understood. I could read *his* thoughts – see the anger simmering behind my brother's eyes. I realized it was something I was going to have to deal with, probably sooner rather than later.

But not yet.

Not while we were still in danger. Not while I was still useful.

I held Jed's gaze, but I couldn't match his intensity. He was grimacing with pain from his swollen jaw, but beneath that agony, his hatred was clear, boiling just below the surface, waiting to erupt.

Harrigan seemed to sense the tension between Jed and me. He looked quizzical. He glanced a question at me but I ignored him.

"Your jaw looks worse," I said to Jed. "More swollen. You look sick."

He didn't say anything for a long while. Then he finally grunted. "It's all right."

"You sure?"

"Yeah."

"Good," I said. "Then as soon as you change into dry clothes, you can pull sentry duty at the back door for a few hours. One of us will relieve you later in the night."

Jed balked – and I sensed bitter words leap into his mouth. But he clamped his jaw shut, simmering, and got to his feet. "I'll start now," he said, and disappeared down the hallway without another word.

Harrigan glanced at me again. "Did I miss something between you two?"

I shook my head. I didn't want to answer – this wasn't the time to go into it – but in the end, I couldn't help myself. Somehow the words just spilled out.

"Jed's going to kill me," I said suddenly, my expression as dark as the night. "My brother is going to kill me as soon as we get to safety."

Harrigan flinched in stunned silence.

He gaped at me. "Are you serious?"

I nodded. "Yes."

"But why?"

I sighed. "It's a long story."

Harrigan leaned forward, and his voice was a hushed conspiratorial whisper. "Are you really serious? You're not making this up?"

"I wish I were," I said, and leaned heavily back against the wall. I stared at Harrigan and held his gaze. "I mean it."

"Why?"

"Because I killed his wife and child," I said, and my gaze went down to the bright little flame of the candle, and my mind drifted back to the first days of the apocalypse. I sighed, seeing the bloody horror in my mind once more – scenes of madness and terror that haunted me in my sleep.

I glanced up at Harrigan. His eyes were wide, his expression confused.

"Jed had been in prison," I said. "Not for anything as simple as stealing candy bars, either. He was there for murder," I said flatly. "It was an armed robbery that went wrong. He shot a man and did eleven hard years. He was released the day before the world went to hell and the zombie virus started sweeping down the east coast." I took a deep breath and then went on. "I was supposed to look after his family while he was inside. He had a wife, and a baby girl. He went to prison before the girl was born. He'd never even seen her. I was taking care of them. I helped with the bills, mowed the lawn – that kind of thing," I said carefully. "I was watching over them until he got out. He was on his way home – taking the overnight bus. I went to the Greyhound station to pick him up – and by the time we got back into town, we could see streets on fire and hear sirens. The cops had the roads blocked off, and the army was moving in a convoy of trucks and armored vehicles. There were helicopters swarming all across the sky. They were strafing the streets.

"We tried to go round the roadblock. We went cross-country, but I crashed the car and we had to hike the rest of the way. It took us three days. By the time we reached his house, they were gone. His wife and child. The door had been broken in – windows smashed. We found blood on the walls, but nothing else."

"Infected?" Harrigan asked softly.

I nodded. "I guess so. Or torn to pieces. I honestly don't know. All I know is they weren't there, and Jed blamed me. He blamed me for not taking them to the depot to meet him. He blamed me for leaving them alone. And then he vowed to kill me."

Harrigan shook his head. "But he never said anything to me. Not in all the time I was in that house with you. Not once. I mean, sure, I saw the way he looked at you sometimes, and I knew he had an attitude, Mitch – but I thought that was just a brotherly thing. You know. I had no idea he wanted you dead. Are you sure he's serious?"

I smiled wryly. "It's family business," I said, and my voice was tight and heavy. "It's a feud. It's between him and me. And yes – I'm sure he's serious."

Again Harrigan shook his head. "But why didn't he kill you there and then?" he asked macabrely. "If he blames you and hates you, why are you still alive?"

"Because we were in the middle of bloody Hell," I said. "He needed me. We found a car and got away. Made it as far south as this town before the car gave out. Made it to the house – and were there ever since. You see, he's waiting. He's waiting until we're clear of the infected areas, or until the army gets control of the plague and starts to fight back. He's waiting until he doesn't need me anymore," I explained. "That's when he's going to kill me."

"But, Mitch. That could be any time. It could be tonight or tomorrow...."

I nodded gravely. "I know," I said, and sighed. "I thought he was going to do it a week ago when you first appeared at the front door of that house, covered in blood. I thought maybe your arrival would be enough to convince him he didn't need me. Now it's something I have to deal with again. This new guy and his daughter – maybe he will think he now has enough support to make it to safety."

There was another long silence. It stretched out between us until finally Harrigan slowly raised his eyes.

"That's why he was suddenly looking at you like he wants you dead?"

I nodded. "Maybe. Maybe he's getting ready – preparing himself for the moment," I said. "Each time we move, he thinks it brings us closer to safety – closer to the time when he can put a bullet in my head and take his revenge for the death of his wife and daughter. Maybe he's out in that kitchen right now, planning my murder."

"Good Lord," Harrigan said in an awed, horrified whisper. He stared at me hard for long seconds. "What are you going to do?"

I shrugged. "Nothing," I said, and then sighed heavily. "The truth is, I don't blame him."

"But... you could..."

"What?" I interrupted, and my tone was harsh – crueler and more abrasive than I had intended. "I could kill him first? Kill Jed?"

Harrigan nodded, but said nothing. He was a Christian, and maybe his own question left him a little ashamed.

The big man lapsed into tense silence, and we stared at each other for a long time. Maybe Harrigan thought I was using those moments to contemplate the idea of murdering my brother – but I wasn't. It was something I had already dwelled on for days – weeks – when we had first stumbled upon the safe house and hidden from the zombie holocaust. God knows I am ashamed to admit that I had thought about it. I'd visualized putting the Glock to the base of Jed's neck when he was sleeping. I'd thought about it constantly, trying to muster the will for a cowardly killing. But in the end, I just couldn't do it. I couldn't kill him in cold blood, and I couldn't summon the terrible hate and desperation needed for even the instant it would require to pull a trigger.

Living with the guilt of my brother's dead family was a weight like a stone. Living with his murder – for that is exactly what it would be – was simply too much.

I shook my head slowly. "I can't," I said at last. I pushed myself away from the wall and stared at the ceiling. "Maybe the zombies will do it – but I can't murder my brother."

Sudden soft noise drew my attention and my eyes snapped towards the hallway. The girl and her father were standing there, faces up lit by the candle cupped in the girl's hands. They had both changed. The man was rolling up the sleeves of a checked shirt, and the girl's slim frame was swallowed up by a thick woolen jumper and slacks that were a couple of sizes too large for her. She looked like a school-kid playing dress-up in her mother's clothes.

She came into the living room shyly and set the candle back on top of the television set. Her hair fell forward over her face and she scraped it back with her fingers and then perched herself on the sofa, legs together, hands tucked nervously between her knees. Her father dropped down to the floor beside her and sighed with weary exhaustion. He thrust out his hand at me.

"Colin Walker," he introduced himself, and then nodded at the girl. "And this is my daughter, Millie."

We shook hands – his grip was firm, like a mechanical claw. "Mitch Logan," I said, and then nodded at Harrigan. "And this is Clinton Harrigan."

The men exchanged nods, and there was a moment of awkward silence. Then Walker glanced in the direction of the darkened hallway. "And who is the big guy? He looks like a thug."

I smiled wryly. "He is," I said, "and he's my brother, Jed."

More awkward silence. Walker cleared his throat. "What's wrong with his face?"

I sighed. "Well, his eyes are too close together, he's got a big nose, and his ears are a weird shape," I said.

Walker frowned. Clearly, the man had no sense of humor.

"No. I mean his jaw."

"Infected tooth," I said. "He's had it for over a week. It's getting worse."

"Have you tried to remove it for him?"

I shook my head. "Have you ever tried wrestling an angry bull? There's no way Jed is going to let anyone touch that tooth."

Walker's expression became more serious. "Well it won't get better by itself," he said flatly. "If it's not removed he's going to get sick. He's probably already got a fever. It will get worse."

Harrigan interrupted, his expression quizzical. "Are you a doctor, Mr Walker?"

The man shook his head. "No, but I was in the military. I did some basic first aid training, and some not-so-basic first aid training. Nothing surgical – just the kind of stuff that might get a man out of trouble."

Harrigan nodded, then lapsed back into thoughtful silence. I stayed silent too. So, Walker was military, or ex-military at least. That made sense, and fitted with my first impressions of him back inside the hull of the wrecked helicopter. He looked like he was about to say more, but then seemed to stop himself.

We sat watching the candle flame for a few moments and then I got to my feet. "Clinton, we need to get out of these wet clothes, otherwise we'll have to deal with pneumonia."

Harrigan got to his feet. My clothes clung to me like a cold clammy second skin. I unwound the strip of cloth I had wrapped around my forearm and peeled off my heavy leather jacket. I wasn't prepared to discard it, so I left it draped over the back of the television and let it drip a wet puddle onto the carpet. Harrigan shrugged out of his heavy coat, and then we carried a candle down the hall towards the bathroom.

There were jeans that didn't fit, shirts that were too big, and pullovers that were too tight. I came back into the kitchen looking like I had been dressed by a blind man from clothes in the children's section of a department store. It was worse for Harrigan. Nothing fitted his big solid frame.

Harrigan found cans of beans in the pantry and a can opener and spoons in the cutlery drawer. Jed was standing by the kitchen window, the curtains drawn an inch apart, and his face pressed close to the glass, watching the moving, swishing shadows of the night. He had a bottle of whisky in his hand. He must have found it in the pantry. I let it go.

"The new guy has some medical experience," I said to the broad shape of my brother's back. He had found time to change out of his sodden clothes into jeans and a t-shirt that stretched across the muscles of his back and shoulders. "He says that infected tooth has to come out, Jed. He says it isn't going to get better, and unless you do something about it, you're likely to get sick. Real sick." I braced myself for the onslaught, like a man who has just prodded a very big snake with a very short stick.

Jed turned slowly round to face me. I could see the swelling around the side of his face quite clearly, even in the light from the candle. His face was dark. It was cold in the room, yet he looked like he was sweating.

Fever.

He cleared his throat and made a hideous face, filled with sudden pain. He nodded. "I know," he said. He was suffering.

I blinked in surprise. "So... you're okay about it?"

"No, I'm not fucking okay about it," he snapped in a voice that was slurred and misshapen by the swelling. "But it's gotta be done. Just not by you." Jed stabbed his finger at me.

I raised my eyebrow. "You don't trust me?"

He shook his head.

"Well the new guy said he was military. He's done some first aid..."

Jed nodded reluctantly. He took a long drink from the whisky bottle. It was already half-empty. He held the sloshing contents up and showed me. "When I've finished this," he said. "It's anesthetic."

I nodded. I glanced at Harrigan, and he followed me back towards the darkened living room.

Walker turned and looked up at me as I came back into the room. "I just spoke to my brother," I said quietly. "He needs that tooth removed. Will you do it?"

Walker nodded. "I overheard the conversation," he said, and then nodded slowly. "Yeah, I'll do it – if you can find me a pair of long-nosed pliers."

Harrigan handed the cans of beans, the can opener, and the cutlery to the girl. She took them without a word.

"This place might have a work shed or a garage," I said. "Maybe out the back. I'll take a look."

I left Harrigan with Walker and his daughter huddled around the candles, and re-traced my steps into the kitchen. Jed heard me. He turned, stared hard at me, but said not a word.

"Anything moving outside?" I asked, nodding at the kitchen window.

Jed sucked in a breath, and grimaced with a sudden flash of pain. "Fucking everything," he said. "The wind is still blowing and the storm is still right overhead. Everything is moving."

I went to the back door. It was locked, with a big brass key still in the key-hole. I unlocked the door and cracked it open. A blast of howling icy wind slapped me in the face. I couldn't see anything. The night was pitch-black.

"Where you going?" Jed asked suddenly.

I glanced at him. "To find something to remove that tooth with," I said.

"From where?"

I shrugged. "There must be a shed or a garage in the back yard," I said. "It's bound to have tools – maybe even things we can use as weapons. I'm going out to take a look."

Jed seemed to freeze for a moment, and I saw his expression change. It was like he was dealing with a split-personality disorder, not knowing which part of him would speak next. Finally he sighed, and stepped close to me. I could smell the fetid stench of his stale breath, mingling with the fumes of the whisky. But his eyes were clear and sharp. He reached into a low kitchen cupboard and handed me a flashlight. It was a long, heavy thing. I hefted it in my hand. It hadn't been there when Harrigan and I had searched the kitchen for food and drink. It was the kind of heavy blunt object that murders were committed with. "Take this," he said reluctantly. "I found it in one of the bedside drawers."

I flicked the flashlight on, and the beam cut through the night like a laser, seemingly brilliant white to my night-adjusted eyes. The flare of light bounced off the kitchen walls, illuminating the entire room. I flicked it off immediately and stared down at it, contemplating.

"You were going to keep this for yourself, right?"

Jed said nothing. He glared at me, his body bristling with defiance.

"You were going to take it when we left the house, but not tell anyone you had it."

Jed said nothing.

I pulled open the door and went out into the night without another word. I snapped the flashlight on for not more than two brief seconds – but it was enough to get my bearings. The light sliced through the driving, misting rain, and cast the back yard of the home under an instant flash like daylight.

There was a small garden shed to my left, set against the side fence of the property. In front of me was level grassy lawn, studded with low trees and shrubs, tied to wooden stakes for support. In the far right corner of the yard was the dark brooding shape of a garage, connected to the side of the house by some kind of a concrete driveway.

The garden shed was closer. The garage in the back corner offered the most likely solution.

I hesitated – and then went left across the lawn towards the tiny garden shed.

It ghosted out of the dark night, and when I felt I must be standing right in front of it, I cupped my hand over the lens of the flashlight to mute the glow and flicked it back on. I was still three feet away from the structure, and I had somehow veered further to my left than I had intended. I was just about to walk into the damned fence.

I finally found the door. It was a thin metal thing with tiny plastic handles – a pair of doors that slid apart. I slid the right-hand door open a couple of inches and clenched my jaw tight as the bottom of the door scraped on broken rollers. I paused – stood perfectly still – and waited for snarling sounds of death to fill the night.

Nothing. Just the howl of the wind and the drumming of the rain on the aluminum roof of the shed. I slid the door open wide enough for me to squeeze into the darkened opening – and kicked a wheelbarrow with my shin.

The shed was tiny – maybe six feet square. I cupped my hand over the lens of the torch once more and switched the flashlight back on.

There was a lawn mower, a couple of cans of fuel, some bags of potting mix and dirt – and a shelf of gardening tools. I snatched at the tools quickly, but nothing looked or felt like pliers.

I flicked the flashlight off and backed out of the shed. I left the door open.

In my mind's-eye I could see the big garage, and I veered back across the sodden muddy lawn towards the rear of the property until I felt hard concrete under my feet and knew I was standing on the driveway. I took short steps until I sensed a solid dark shape before me. Again, I used the flashlight only briefly. I was in front of a roller-door.

The garage was wide enough for a single car. I skirted round the side of the structure carefully and found a door. It was locked. I tried the handle, and leaned my shoulder against it, but it remained stubbornly shut. I went back to the roller door and felt until my fingers found the handle and lock. I lifted. The door rolled up effortlessly – and silently. I lifted it no more than a couple of feet and then lay on the wet concrete and crawled into the dark cavernous space.

The sound of the rain on the roof was deafening. The garage was empty. I smelled oil and fuel, but there was no vehicle. I flicked the flashlight on and swept the harsh beam of light swiftly around the interior.

The garage was the kind of place where a very bored, or very old man spent his time. It was organized with military precision. Against the far wall was a sturdy timber work bench with a vice, and a drill on some kind of a metal frame. The wall was covered in all manner of tools, each item hung on hooks, within a painted outline, so that every piece went back in the right place and could be accounted for.

On the side wall were several shelves of small cardboard boxes, each stacked neatly. I figured they held nails and screws, but I didn't waste time investigating.

I went to the back wall. There wasn't one pair of pliers – there were four. There was a long-nosed pair of pliers, a standard pair, a miniature pair, and an extra large pair that looked like the brutal instrument of some medieval torturer. I took them all, and went back out under the roller door, back out into the rain and the dark night. I slid the roller door down until it was closed, and followed the concrete driveway until I sensed I was near the corner of the house. I had my hands full with tools and the flashlight and so it took me a minute to juggle everything until I could flick the light back on for one final second to orientate myself. The light burst bright across the back of the house and I caught a split-second glimpse of Jed's dark scowling face in the gloom behind the kitchen curtains. I went to the back door, soaking wet again, and shivering from the cold and the tension.

I stood in the kitchen for long seconds, catching my breath as water dripped onto the floor.

"Find anything?" Jed's voice ghosted out of the night. He was still by the window.

"Yeah," I said, and set the array of tools down on the kitchen counter. "I'm sure one of these will do the job."

There was a moment of silence, then Jed said softly, "Jesus." He took another long urgent mouthful of whisky. The bottle was less than a third full. I left the flashlight on the counter beside the pliers. "We'll be needing the strong light when Walker rips your tooth out," I said with a hint of malicious pleasure. "We wouldn't want him to wrench out the wrong one – would we?"

I left Jed, and used the cigarette lighter to find the bathroom where I changed into more dry clothes, before heading back into the living room.

I could hear a soft murmuring voice, and when I reached the doorway, I saw Colin Walker leaning close to the candles, his hands splayed wide, and his facial features intense. He was talking quietly to Harrigan, who seemed genuinely appalled. Harrigan heard me approach and his head snapped round. His eyes were wide and fearful.

"Mitch, come and listen to this," he urged. "Mr Walker – he has information about the virus."

I sat down. The candle light guttered and then came back, glowing brightly.

Colin Walker looked at me and raised an eyebrow.

I nodded. "I found four pairs of pliers. I'm sure one of them will do," I said. "I left them in the kitchen – and Jed found a flashlight."

Walker nodded, then started to get to his feet but I grabbed his arm, and he sank slowly back to the floor. "Jed's still got about a third of a bottle of whisky to go," I said. "Maybe another thirty minutes. By then he'll be feeling no pain."

Walker relaxed a little. Harrigan cut across the conversation. "Tell Mitch what you told me," he urged. "Tell him what you know about the undead virus."

Walker's eyes flicked back to me and he stared hard. His gaze was steady – almost disconcerting.

"I was a janitor in Washington," he said quietly. "I worked for the Government."

I frowned. "I thought you were military."

"I was," he said. "But when I mustered out after the Middle East, there wasn't a lot of work for guys like me. So I took the only work available," his eyes shifted to glance at the silhouette of his daughter sitting quietly in the sofa chair, and then back to me. "When the virus first hit, the government didn't know how it started," Walker went on. "They still don't. They don't know if it was from one of our CDC labs – an experiment that went horribly wrong – or whether it was an act of international terrorism."

"Terrorism?"

Walker nodded. "A dozen militant terrorist groups claimed responsibility for the virus. Every extreme group you have ever heard of, and plenty more you wouldn't know about. They all claimed the virus as their own, and said it was Allah's Wrath against the Great Satan... you know the kind of things they say."

I sat in complete silence. Jed and I had been holed up in a house for three weeks, with no contact to the outside world. The only snatches of news we had heard had been during the first few days of frantic fractured radio grabs as we drove to escape the plague. Since then, we'd heard nothing, and seen very little. During the first week in the safe house, we had seen undead roaming the street beyond the front window. We'd seen two cars crash, and the victims set upon and

95

dragged from their vehicles. We had seen the victims torn to pieces and their bodies dismembered. But the horror had been isolated and localized to what was going on outside that window. We had no idea that the entire country had gone to hell.

"How far has it spread?" I asked quietly.

"Everywhere," Walker said. "It spread like a wild-fire, starting somewhere here on the east coast. One rumor was that the virus had been brought into America by an infected Egyptian sailor who arrived in Baltimore harbor with unusual symptoms... but no one really knows," Walker said. "But within days it had raged along the entire east coast, and before the Government could develop some way to quarantine the affected states, it had spread west. The whole country is gone," Walker's voice became grave. He shook his head. "It's all gone."

The news was like a punch in the guts. Isolated, Jed and I had dared to hope that somehow our Government was working hard to contain the spread of the infection. I thought maybe the military was flexing its muscle and preparing to sweep back up the coast, reclaiming the areas that had been infected. We thought hope and help were still somewhere nearby, and that all we needed to do was wait for the cavalry to sweep back into Virginia and restore order – that one day soon this would all be over and we could pick up the pieces of our lives. We thought the world would go on. Now I realized suddenly that it wouldn't.

The world would never be the same again. Fear and horror were the new everyday reality. We weren't victims of some terrible natural disaster – we were the survivors of an apocalyptic plague.

I shook my head in disbelief. "The Government...?"

"There isn't one," Walker said bluntly. "And there's no army. It's like every worse-case nuclear scenario you could imagine," he said darkly. "There are pockets of survivors, but chaos reigns. The undead virus has wiped out everything. Social order collapsed within the first week. Since then it has just gotten worse."

Harrigan interrupted. "You said there were survivors. What do you mean?"

Walker stared down into the light of the candle and his voice became low and heavy.

"The navy has ships off the coast. They were recalled from their station in the Mediterranean once things got out of hand. The infection hasn't reached them. They're offshore, taking any survivors who can reach them."

I shook my head. It made no sense. "And how the hell do people reach the ships?"

Walker made a macabre, bleak face. "There is a staging point about forty miles south of here. It's a little town on the coast called Pentelle. Somehow, it has remained virus free. There are troops there."

I stared off into the darkness.

Forty miles.

It might as well be a million. The chances of us ever making the distance through a world filled with undead killers were practically zero.

"The only other way… is by helicopter," Walker said, and there was a pointed bitter emphasis to his words.

Harrigan picked up the ball. "And that's where you and your daughter were heading?"

Walker nodded. "The plan was to fly to Pentelle," he said softly. "There was a pilot flying people out of the Capitol. He was charging twenty grand for a seat on his chopper."

I sat and thought for long seconds. "Is that why the helicopter was painted black?"

Walker shrugged. "I suppose," he said, as though it had never been something he had considered. "This guy was making a fortune. He was ferrying the wealthy and the desperate. He didn't care."

I did some more thinking, and then shook my head slowly. "We never heard another helicopter," I said. "Ever. If this guy was flying people from the Capitol to this place on the coast, why didn't we hear him flying overhead? He must have been making several flights a day. It's probably only a two hundred and fifty mile flight."

"We got into trouble," Walker explained. "We should have been east of here. The route was along the coast. But shortly after liftoff, there were engine problems. At first I thought the pilot was scamming us – trying to get extra money. But he wasn't. The instrument panel went haywire, and suddenly we were flying miles off course. He was fighting just to keep the thing in the air. That's how we ended up here – and it's the reason we crashed."

"You were lucky to survive," Harrigan said gently.

Walker said nothing for a long moment, then he looked up at Harrigan's ruddy face. "Were we?" he asked softly, then shook his head. "I prayed that if we crashed, we died instantly – because that death would be better than being torn apart by the undead."

Solemn silence. My thoughts went back to the dead bodies littered across the grass just a few hundred yards back down the street, and to the scene Jed had described as the undead ghouls had reached the helicopter and torn the pilot's body apart.

"Do you know anything about the virus?" I asked Walker. "How it spreads? How it affects the victims? How to stop them?"

Walker took a deep breath and frowned in dark concentration. "It's bad," he said. "Real bad. If you're asking me what the scientists call the virus, I honestly couldn't tell you. It's got a name about twenty-seven letters long. But in Washington – and on the streets – they're calling it the Jaws Virus."

"Jaws?"

Walker nodded.

"What does that stand for?" Harrigan asked.

"Nothing," Walker said darkly. "It's not an acronym. It's because of the way the virus makes the undead act. They're like sharks," he said. "Their hearing seems to be greatly magnified, so that movement attracts them – just like a shark. And the blood. They sense it. It drives them to frenzy," he explained. "The thirst for blood is the trigger. That is why not everyone bitten is infected and becomes another undead killer," he said. "Because sometimes they just tear the body to pieces. Sometimes they're so driven to a frenzy that they turn upon themselves. If they're still fresh – still in the early stages of infection – a wound to themselves can be enough to drive others around them to madness. They turn on the victim. That's what we saw tonight, when you shot that tall undead man, and he went over backwards near the helicopter. He must have been fresh. There must still have been blood in his body. The others sensed it immediately and tore him to pieces. That's why you can't ever get a wound and leave it unattended. They sense it somehow. And that's why it has been called Jaws – because of Spielberg's shark movie."

"How do we kill them?"

"Head shot," Walker said. "It's the only way."

I grunted, and remembered the ghoul that had attacked Harrigan on the rain swept street. I remembered the instant when Jed's bullet had torn through the zombie's eye socket after we had shot it repeatedly in the chest with absolutely no effect. "We figured as much out for ourselves," I said. 'We just had to find out the hard way."

"The hard way?" Walker asked.

"Trial and error," I said vaguely.

I sat back out of the candle light and arranged my thoughts. There were a lot of questions I wanted to ask Walker. For all he had told us about the virus, the man himself – and his daughter –remained mysteries. We knew nothing about them, and it left me feeling uneasy. But a sudden sound from the kitchen snapped my senses to full alertness. I got to my feet, my hand going instinctively to the Glock, and whirled round, just in time to see my brother stagger into the living room. The bottle of whisky was clutched in his big knuckled hand. It was empty. Jed swayed on unsteady feet, looking like a dark deathly apparition. He stared blankly for long seconds, rocking from side to side like a man on a small boat in a storm.

"Fucker!" he hissed at me, "let's get this over and fucking done with." Then he seemed to recognize the shape of Walker's teenage daughter huddled down deep in the cushions of the sofa, and he was overcome by some ridiculous attempt at manners. "Fuck. Sorry," he mangled an apology. "I fucking forgot about you."

The girl said nothing. Walker and Harrigan got to their feet. Walker glanced at me. "We'll do it in the bathroom," he said. "It will be easier to clean up afterwards."

I nodded. "Will there be blood?"

Walker's face twisted into some kind of a smile. "Oh, yes," he said. "There will be blood."

Walker turned to his daughter. "Stay here, Millie."

She sat up with sudden alarm. "No!" she blurted, and there was a flush of fear beneath the skin of her cheeks. She was terrified of being alone. "I... I want to stay with you," she said softly, and then added, "Dad."

There were a couple of straight-backed chairs nested around a table in the kitchen. I carried one of them through to the bathroom and set it down on the tiled floor near the vanity sink. Walker had two pairs of pliers in his hands, and Harrigan gave me the flashlight and stood back. Jed slumped down onto the chair, and his head lolled to the side. His eyes were bleary and unfocussed. There were little frothy bubbles of spittle at the corners of his mouth.

There was just one small window in the bathroom and we had drawn the curtains shut when we had first cleared the house. Now Harrigan hung heavy towels over the opening so that we could use the flashlight without fear. I flicked it on. The light was dazzling – a piercing beam that bounced off the white tiles of the walls and floor, and illuminated the whole room.

Walker chose the long-nosed pliers and tested them, snapping at thin air. They looked vile and menacing, and the serrated grip was crusted with dirt. He cleaned them on the tail of his shirt and looked at Harrigan.

"You'll have to hold him down," Walker said. "Get behind him and pin his arms."

Harrigan looked doubtful. He was a big man, but Jed was bigger and more finely muscled. And Jed had a temper. Harrigan hesitated. "Shouldn't.... shouldn't we tie him down?"

I shook my head. "No rope," I said. "And I'm not going back out into the night to find any."

Still Harrigan hesitated. He edged himself behind the chair and took up a position where he could press down on Jed's shoulders. Walker snatched another towel from a railing and wrapped it across Jed's chest, like a hairdresser's cape.

"For the blood," he explained to me – not that he needed to.

I leaned close to Jed and looked him in the eye. We were gathered in a tight knot around the chair and Jed was beginning to look alarmed. He knew what was coming – and the imminent fear of pain was starting to seep through the whiskey-fueled haze.

"You can't make any noise," I said to Jed, speaking slowly and clearly to make sure he understood. "It's important," I explained. "The undead are like sharks, Jed. They hear noise – it sounds the same as someone splashing in the water does to a shark – so if you start screaming, they are going to hear you. They'll find us and kill us all. Understand?"

Jed nodded, but it was a jerky, spasmodic gesture that spoke of his fear. He was tense in the chair. I could see the thick corded veins in his neck beginning to swell. His jaw was clenched tightly shut. Walker leaned over him.

"Open up," he said.

Jed hesitated. His eyes flicked to me, then up to the ceiling. His mouth opened reluctantly.

"Wider."

Jed made a sharp hissing sound through his nostrils, like a bull about to charge. I turned the flashlight round and shone the bright light into his mouth.

Walker hunched down a little and his voice became perfunctory and practical. I crouched down close beside him. Jed's breath stank. It smelled like a skunk had crawled between his lips and died. Walker reversed the pliers in his hand.

They had a yellow plastic grip. He eased them inside Jed's mouth and rested the edge of his hand on Jed's bottom jaw to stop him slamming his mouth shut. Using one handle of the pliers, Walker gently tapped at a lower back tooth that was barely visible, surrounded by infected red swollen gum.

"Is this the one?" He touched the tooth – and Jed's body went stiff with an electric jolt of pain. His hands clawed at the armrests of the chair and he thumped his foot on the floor. Harrigan jumped in alarm and locked his big beefy hands down on Jed's shoulders, clamping like a vice.

Jed wailed in low pain and said something that was distorted by the shape of his mouth.

Walker straightened and turned to me. "It's nasty," he said. "Very nasty. The gum is swollen so that it will be hard to get a grip on the tooth." He looked thoughtful, and then bent back down to look inside Jed's open mouth again.

"See the tooth?" he asked. I peered over the rim of the flashlight. "See the cavity in the middle? That's going to make it tough to get a good grip with the pliers," Walker explained. "Because if I grab too hard, the tooth might shatter completely."

I raised an eyebrow. "Is that bad?"

"Very," he said. "Then I'd have to dig around, trying to remove the broken fragments. We could be here for hours, and I might not get it all."

I caught a glimpse of Jed's expression. He was going white. The blood was draining from his face, and his eyes were wide, rolling in their sockets with absolute terror.

"Jesus," he said in a quiet, fearful whisper.

Jed was a big guy, and he had spent over a decade in one of the country's toughest prisons. He was as hard as nails – utterly fearless and grim-faced in the fiercest fight – and yet here he was, confronted with having a simple tooth extracted, and he was on the verge of sheer blind panic.

I concealed a grin of pure enjoyment.

"But can't you just grab the top between the pincers and yank it out?" I asked. I saw Jed flinch. He was trembling. His eyes rolled from side to side, following the conversation as Walker and I stood over him.

"Oh, hell no," Walker said. "That is the worst thing you can do. I saw a buddy try that in the field when I was in the Middle East," he said, delighting in recalling the details. "A guy's tooth had become infected, and we were miles from base. My buddy tried to get the tooth out with a little pair of pincers. He practically had to put his knee on the guy's chest." Walker shook his head. "No, no, no. You see there's roots and all kinds of gristle around the tooth, so you've got to grip it, then push down hard. Then you twist the pliers one way then back the other way. Then you pull." Walker made a graphic demonstration with the pliers, close to Jed's face.

Jed sat bolt upright. "No fucking way!" he hissed.

I turned on him. "Quiet!" I snapped. "Remember, the zombies have incredible hearing. Any sound from you is going to bring them down on us and we'll all be killed."

105

"Better that than this," Jed growled. "Christ almighty, you bastards are fixing to kill me."

"Quiet!"

Jed threw himself back into the chair, muttering darkly and dangerously. Walker leaned over him again, and Jed's mouth fell open, showing dull yellow teeth. "Might as well get it over and done with, I guess."

I leaned in close, holding the flashlight steady. Walker eased the pincers around the top of the tooth and took up the pressure. His brow was furrowed in concentration. I saw Jed's throat begin to convulse as if he was trying to swallow. Behind him, Harrigan was almost as white-faced as Jed. He clamped his hands down on my brother's shoulders and clung on.

Walker got the pliers in place. Jed's whole body was rigid as a board.

"There," I said solicitously. "Now that doesn't hurt, does it?"

Jed made a sound in the back of his throat but it was indecipherable. Walker took up the pressure – and then stopped suddenly. He glanced at me. "Did you find any salt when you searched the kitchen?"

I blinked. "I think so," I said slowly, remembering. "I think there's some in the pantry. Why?"

"There is going to be a lot of blood," Walker said. "Most likely it's going to spray everywhere, and there will be yellow oozing puss from the infection. If the tooth doesn't shatter completely, and we yank it out in one piece, it would be helpful for your brother to rinse his mouth in salty water for a day or two."

I nodded.

Jed groaned. His face was beginning to sheen in fearful beads of perspiration – and then before I realized it, Walker seemed to lean his body forward and press down hard on the handles of the pliers.

Jed started to keen – a wailing, moaning noise of terrible pain, a sound low in the back of his throat but rising higher. Walker changed his grip. He twisted the pliers and I heard a sound like bone breaking. Then he quickly reversed the action, twisting in the opposite direction.

Blood and puss gushed across Jed's tongue and spilled over his lip. The sound of his agony became a sound like a kettle boiling. Then Walker pulled back on the pliers and Jed's pain became a long terrible moan.

For long seconds nothing happened. I could see Harrigan struggling to keep Jed still in the chair. His knuckles were turning white. Jed started to strain. He lashed out with his leg and his big hands balled into clenched fists. He pounded them on the armrest, and I saw the look of murderous rage blazing in his eyes.

Then I heard another *'crack!'* – a distinctive sound above the pained noise – and the pliers slid from Jed's mouth, gripped around a huge decayed tooth with tattered shreds of flesh and root clumped around it. Blood gushed, flooding down Jed's chin and spattering across the towel, and he reeled away, broke free of Harrigan's powerful grip, and lunged to his feet, one hand slapped across his jaw, and the other bunched into a fist the size of a sledge-hammer.

"Bastards!" Jed hissed – and more blood spilled down his chin. The towel fell to the floor. He kicked it away and then bent double with pain. I glanced urgently at Harrigan. We had about three seconds to escape the bathroom before Jed turned his blazing anger onto anything – or anyone – within reach.

"Everyone out!" I said urgently. I could quite easily have said 'run for your life!'

Jed's temper was like a volcano. I'd seen him erupt before. We scrambled through the bathroom door while he was bent over, moaning in pain, and I slapped Harrigan on the shoulder. "Grab hold of that door handle and don't let go for the next five minutes," I said.

It was fifteen minutes before I finally got up the nerve to go into the bathroom. Jed was pale-faced, grim, leaning over the bathroom vanity, staring at his reflection in the mirror. The murderous blaze of anger in his eyes had died. He turned and glared at me. I handed him a plastic bottle of water I had poured salt into.

"Rinse," I said.

The bathroom looked like murder had been done. There was blood spattered on the floor and on the sink, and more blood on the towel. Jed took the bottle from me without a word. His eyes were clear and steady, and it looked already as though some of the swelling had gone from around his jaw. He took a swig from the water bottle and spat a bloody mess into the sink.

"You okay?" I asked.

Jed looked at me hard, and his lips compressed into a thin pale line. "Fucker," he said.

Walker leaned in through the open bathroom door and surveyed the area. "We had better clean this up," he said. "Just in case."

I looked alarmed. "What? Could zombies pick up the scent of Jed's blood – through walls?"

Walker shrugged. "I don't know," he confessed. "Maybe. Maybe if they were outside the house…" his voice trailed off. He didn't sound like he believed it. "But there's no point taking chances."

I rinsed the blood away and wiped down the walls and floor. Harrigan helped me. Walker took Jed back into the living room and by the time Harrigan and I had rejoined the group, Jed was asleep on the floor, snoring.

It was late. Outside the storm seemed to be finally exhausting itself. We could still hear rain spattering against the windows, and the low mournful moan of the wind through the nearby tree tops, but for all that, the elements seemed to have lost their venom.

I looked at Walker. His daughter was asleep, curled up into a ball on the sofa like a kitten. "You should get some rest," I said. "Harrigan and I will stand guard during the night."

Walker bridled at that. He shook his head. "I can pull my weight," he said with dogged resolve. "I've got military training. I'm used to long hours and long nights on sentry duty."

I nodded slowly. "I'm sure you are," I said carefully. "But you've been in a helicopter crash, you have a bump the size of a golf ball on your head… and, quite frankly, I don't trust you yet."

His eyes snapped to mine, and went hard as stone.

"What did you say?"

"I said I don't trust you," I measured my words and tone carefully. "It's nothing personal. It's just how things are. We don't know a damned thing about you, Mr Walker – and until we do, I'm not willing to put my life in your hands."

His expression became flinty. "But you expect me to trust you?"

"No," I said, and got to my feet. "That's your choice. You've always got the option of leaving. The front door is right there."

* * *

I took one of the candles with me, and went out into to the kitchen for the first watch. My thoughts were black and bitter. Dark depression filled me, for I had a strange sense of impending disaster. It was like a heavy blanket draped across my shoulders – I just couldn't shake the feeling off. Common sense told me it was a reaction to the stress, the fear and sheer exhaustion – but a tiny warning voice of instinct wouldn't go away.

My thoughts started swirling in an unbreakable circle, going over the same questions, the same doubts. It was like trying to catch smoke. There was nothing substantial to grasp, and I realized I would get nowhere without more information about Colin Walker. Eventually I gave up.

Some time in the early hours of the morning, Harrigan appeared at my shoulder, silent as a ghost. I was at the curtained window, staring hard through a chink in the material at the night, watching the trees swaying until the storm finally blew itself out and the darkness became eerily calm and silent.

"Anything?"

I shook my head. "Nothing," I said.

There was a can of soda on the kitchen counter that I had been drinking from, and beside it an empty can of beans. Harrigan picked up the soda and drank thirstily until it was empty. He burped.

"What do you think about Walker?" Harrigan asked me.

I shook my head. "I don't know," I admitted. "I just have this feeling about the guy. Something doesn't add up."

Harrigan said nothing for a long moment and we stood in the silence both staring out into the night. I watched the big man's face out of the corner of my eye. He looked thoughtful.

"Maybe you're judging him unkindly," Harrigan said at last. "Trust is a two-way street, Mitch – and in fairness, you've told him nothing at all about who we are. Maybe that would be a good place to start." His tone was gentle and placatory – but still I felt my anger rising. "As the Good Book says…"

I rounded on him. Perhaps it was because he had a point, or perhaps it was because the last thing I needed right then was another one of Harrigan's sermons. Clinton was a good man, but his sense of Christian faith and charity were diametrically opposed to my instincts for survival.

"You turned up at the safe house unarmed, covered in blood and carrying a Bible, Clinton. And it took me three days before I felt I could trust you. Walker was in a crashed helicopter with a dead pilot and a teenage daughter. And a gun. He says he's an ex-military janitor, and that he bought two seats to freedom for twenty grand each. Now, how many janitors do you know that have a lazy forty thousand dollars conveniently laying around their house at the precise moment the apocalypse sweeps across the country?"

I had other suspicions about Colin Walker too – ones I didn't mention to Harrigan right then, but fears nonetheless that troubled me deeply. Little things. Big things.

Perhaps they were all just a result of my own paranoia.

Harrigan took a step back. Maybe he was surprised at the extent of my sudden anger. His expression went blank.

"And the girl bothers me," I went on, mollifying my tone just a little and keeping my voice to a hoarse whisper. "She hasn't said two words since we rescued them. Doesn't that strike you as a little unusual?"

Harrigan's brow furrowed. "She's scared, Mitch. After all she has been through tonight, I would think it's perfectly normal."

I raised my eyebrow to make the point. "Exactly," I said. "She is scared, Clinton. She's scared shitless – but of who? Is she scared of us, scared of the zombies – or scared of her father?"

* * *

I came awake slowly. It was still dark, and I lay there for long moments, listening to the sounds around me. Jed was nearby – I could hear him still snoring softly. I rolled onto my back and stared at the ceiling.

It was light enough to see cracks and flaked paint around the light fitting. I turned my head and looked at the full-length window near the front door. The curtains were still drawn tight, but there was a soft halo of light around the edges. It was morning.

Another day in an undead world.

I sat up.

Colin Walker was sitting on the living room floor, and his daughter was beside him. The girl had her legs folded beneath her in that distinctly feminine way that only a woman can manage. They were both eating from open cans of cold spaghetti, and there was a can of soda on the ground between them. Walker's gun was resting in his lap.

They looked up at me, stared for a moment, then turned their attention silently back to their food.

I heard Harrigan's heavy footsteps in the hallway and looked round just as he entered the room.

"Morning," he said, his tone polite but brusque. He handed me back my Glock, which I had left with him throughout his stint of sentry duty.

"Morning," I said, and scraped my hands down my face, feeling weary and worn. The stubble on my jaw and chin cracked and crackled under my fingers. "Any idea what time it is?"

Harrigan shrugged. "Sunrise was a few hours ago," he said, making a face like he was considering the question carefully. "So... maybe nine o'clock."

I got to my feet slowly. My body was stiff and sore. I hobbled to the window and edged the curtain open an inch.

It was a blindingly bright summer's morning – so bright it hurt my eyes. The sky was clear brilliant blue. Across the street, the narrow fringe of nature strip we had run through the night before stood like a dappled green wall, beyond which I could just see the pointed roofs of houses. One of them was the safe house we had spent the last three weeks in.

The road between the house and the nature strip was empty, and still damp from the storm, glistening in the sunlight. It was as if the rain had washed the world shiny new and clean.

But I knew that wasn't the case.

I let the curtain fall back into place and turned round to face the group. Jed was making soft throaty sounds. I nudged him with my foot. He grunted, then came awake in a single instant, his eyes sharp and alert.

"We need to make a plan," I stated the obvious. "Clearly, we can't wait here until help arrives. Based on what Walker told us last night, help isn't going to come – ever. So we have to help ourselves. Sooner or later we are going to have to strike out and find other survivors – maybe find a safe place that hasn't been affected by the virus," I paused and swept my eyes across the faces before me. Everyone seemed somber. "But before we do anything, we need to check this house again. We have to go from room to room, gathering everything that might be useful, but nothing that will slow us down. My guess is that we missed plenty last night when we cleared the house. Today we'll find it."

It certainly wasn't a Churchillian speech. No one got to their feet and applauded. Everyone sat in bleak, listless silence. I glanced at Jed.

"How do you feel?"

He nodded. "Better," he said grudgingly. He ran his tongue around the inside of his mouth and then rubbed the side of his face with his hand. The swelling had almost completely gone. He dragged his hands through his hair and opened and closed his mouth a few times, like a man making sure his jaw was still hinged after being punched. He got to his feet and went down the hallway towards the kitchen.

I turned back to Colin Walker. The man's eyes swung to mine like the double-barrels of a shotgun. He was wary.

I forced a smile. "It was pointed out to me last night that we know very little about you, Mr Walker, but that you know even less about us," I said, glancing at Harrigan's suddenly smug expression as I spoke. "Let me fix that right now."

I crossed the living room and held out my hand. "Nice to meet you," I said. Walker reached up and we shook hands, suspicion still creasing his features.

"My name is Mitch Logan. Up until a few weeks ago, I owned a small appliance store in Forresterville. It's a little town about thirty miles north of here. I sold refrigerators and television sets, and I had two sales staff helping me and an office girl. None of them survived the plague," I shook my head with genuine sadness. "And if I live to reach my next birthday I'll be thirty seven years old. I'm single, but not by choice. My wife divorced me three years ago and I hope like Hell that the dragon-slaying horror bitch was dead and mutilated by the first wave of the zombie plague – but knowing my luck, she will have survived, only to bite them back."

I stepped away, turning to Harrigan. "Now you," I said. "Since you're the one who thought we needed this little love-fest."

Was I being sarcastic?

Yep, it was. Harrigan's self-congratulatory little smile slipped from the corners of his mouth.

He introduced himself to Walker and nodded his head politely to his daughter, like a refined gentleman might, back in the days before the Civil War.

"My name is Clinton Harrigan," he cleared his throat and stood quite straight. "And before the terrible plague, I owned the town bakery," he said. "I was married, but my wife was killed by the undead when we tried to escape into the country. We were never blessed with any children."

I watched Walker's face carefully, but his expression never changed. He would have made the perfect poker player.

"You don't have a gun, Mr Harrigan?" Walker asked, and he sounded bewildered.

Harrigan shook his head. "No, sir, I don't. I carry a crow-bar and a Bible. They are my weapon and my shield, along with God's infinite grace and mercy."

Walker said nothing. He rolled his eyes to me. I nodded.

"Mr Harrigan is our resident devout Christian," I confirmed, making my voice sound bright and conversational. "But not the kind that will beat you over the head with Bible quotes until your ears bleed." Then I paused for a beat.

"Not if he knows what's good for him."

Walker nodded. "And what about your brother?"

Jed was still out in the kitchen. I could hear him rummaging through cupboards. I shrugged. "Jed is two years younger than me," I said, "and what you see is exactly what you get. You're a smart enough man to work out the rest, I'm sure."

Again Walker nodded.

He glanced at his daughter then back to me. "So what now?"

I forced another tight smile. "Now you take the gun from your lap and put it in your pocket. It makes me kind of nervous. I'm sure you understand. Then we start searching the house in the spirit that Mr Harrigan here believes we should – with choir music in the background and little blue-birds on our shoulders as new-found

117

life-long friends... for as long as life lasts." And then I muttered dryly, "Praise the Lord."

Harrigan's face became a dark brooding scowl. He was annoyed that I was mocking him, but he still couldn't resist the compulsion.

"Amen," he said softly.

* * *

We couldn't all search the house – it would be madness not to keep a watch posted in case undead drifted nearby, so I split us into two groups. Walker, Jed and I would search every room, while Harrigan and the girl would stay in the living room and stand guard at the front door.

Most of the rooms were at the back of the house and I figured Jed, Walker and I could cover those windows while we were looking for anything that might be of use.

This caused the girl to go into a meltdown. Her eyes welled with tears and her face lost all of its color until she looked pale and white as a ghost. Her lower lip began to tremble, and her fingers began to fiddle anxiously with the chunky bracelet around her wrist, until finally Walker took her aside and spoke to her for several minutes in quiet whispers.

The girl had been completely traumatized by the helicopter crash. The idea of being even in a different part of the house than her father sent her over the edge, and it took a lot of patient coaxing before she finally relaxed enough to follow

Harrigan, timid and reluctant, to the big full-length window.

I left my gun with Harrigan and snatched up the nylon bag. There were a couple of full water bottles and a few cans of beans rolling around in the bottom. I left them on the living room floor.

"This shouldn't take long," I said to Harrigan, but I was talking for the girl's benefit. "Maybe half an hour. We just need to be thorough. We can't afford to miss anything that might be useful."

Harrigan nodded. He twitched the curtain aside half-an-inch and peered out at the bright morning, then glanced back over his shoulder at me. "Take your time," he said casually. "If we see anything, or hear anything, I'll send Millie to fetch you."

"Sounds like a plan," I grunted. I slung the empty bag over my shoulder and followed after Jed and Walker.

We went to the kitchen first.

The first thing I did was check the window, and I spent thirty seconds just standing still and watching the back yard through a crack in the curtains. Under a bright sunny sky the lawns looked much smaller than I had thought. Last night, when I had been staggering in the dark and rain from the garden shed to the garage, it had felt like they were on opposite sides of a football field.

I watched the trees, then ran my eyes along the line of the fence, looking for telltale signs of movement. I saw nothing. Nothing at all, and finally relaxed enough to turn my back on the window and fix my attention on the task at hand.

"Jed, you start with the pantry," I said. It was a big double-door thing. Last night we had found cans of food and soda, and Jed had found the bottle of whisky. But the shelves looked well stocked and badly organized. Maybe there would be other useful items that would turn up with a thorough search.

Jed didn't acknowledge me. He simply started pulling things from the shelves, holding each one up, turning it in his hand, and sorting the contents into useful – and useless.

I started on the kitchen drawers below the sink. Every house has these drawers. The top one holds the cutlery, and the other two or three are always crammed with the assorted junk that doesn't belong anywhere else. I started on the bottom drawer and worked my way up.

Walker stood back in the middle of the room for a moment with his hands on his hips, his gaze thoughtful, his eyes narrowed. He made a face, and then went for the stove. There was a range hood built into the cupboards above the hotplates to draw away cooking smoke and odors. Walker pulled the range hood apart, and behind the mesh filters found almost a thousand dollars wrapped in plastic and bound with a rubber band.

Clever hiding place.

Even more clever of Colin Walker to think of it.

He held the money up triumphantly and counted it quickly. It wasn't a lot of use – unless we needed to light a fire. I didn't imagine money had much value in a world where food, fuel and alcohol would probably be the new currencies.

The nylon bag was open on the kitchen floor near where I was crouched. Walker threw the money in, and started on the row of cupboards above the kitchen bench top.

Despite ten minutes of patient searching, the results were meager. Jed had found more cans of food on an upper shelf – mainly condensed soups and spaghetti – but not much else. Walker's search had been fruitless, and I had found a roll of duct tape and a blister pack of six fresh batteries for the flashlight.

I looked up at the others. "We'll try the main bedroom next," I said.

Strangely, when I pushed the door to the room open, I smelled nothing. It was as if the dead bodies of the man and the woman slumped across the mattress had no stench. I knew that wasn't the reality. The reality was that we had become so accustomed to the thick rancid smell drifting through the house that we no longer noticed. That was a good thing.

There was an antique chest of drawers set against the left wall of the room. It was a beautiful piece of furniture with ornate iron handles on every drawer, and a large oval mirror set into the woodwork. The timber had been varnished and polished to bring out the natural grain.

I started on the top drawers and worked my way down.

Jed slid open the doors of the wardrobe. We had been through the clothes racks the night before, snatching anything dry and tossing it on the floor outside the bathroom. Now he started looking more carefully, digging his hands into the pockets of coats that hung in the corners, and slinging any garments that looked practical over his shoulder for later inspection.

Walker dropped to his stomach and slid underneath the bed. I knew he would find the little revolver the couple had shot themselves with, because I had seen it and decided to leave it when we first found the bodies. But I didn't mention I knew the weapon was there. I waited and listened carefully as I searched.

And I wondered.

The top few drawers of the dresser were filled with cosmetics, nylon stockings and underwear. Lots of underwear, mainly of the flimsy, lacy type. One drawer held the family's important papers. There were laminated certificates, something that looked like a wad of stock shares, and passports. I didn't open them. I didn't want to know the names of the people.

I slid open the bottom drawer and froze with a sudden sense of amusement and perverse voyeurism. The draw was filled with 'marital aids'. Apart from a couple of battery-operated devices, there was a length of soft rope, a blindfold and a pair of handcuffs. The cuffs were silver, and there was a key on a small length of ribbon. The end of the key was decorated with an ornate love heart. I pulled everything from the drawer and set it on the bedroom floor. I wanted the batteries, and the rope and cuffs were the first really useful discovery we had made. Jed made the sound of a low whistle.

"Jesus," he said, and his eyes were suddenly alive and cunning. "Looks like someone read 'Fifty Shades' before they ate a bullet.

I nodded. "Maybe that's what drove them to kill themselves," I said wryly.

Walker wriggled back out from under the bed. He saw the array of items gathered around me but said nothing. I unwound the rope. It was about fifteen feet long. Useful indeed. I gave the handcuffs a quick test. They were toys. I had thought they were metal, but they were made of heavy plastic. Useless after all. I ripped the batteries from the adult toys. They weren't the right size for the flashlight, but I felt they might still be useful. I threw them into the nylon bag, then looked up at Walker.

He had the little revolver in one hand, and a half-opened box of ammunition in the other.

I was secretly relieved he had passed the test.

"This was beside the bed," he said. "It's the weapon they used. One shot each. There are four rounds left in the cylinder, and about twenty rounds left in the box. It was under the bed."

"Is it any use to us?" I asked. The weapon looked tiny compared to my Glock, and the cannon that Walker carried.

He shrugged. "It will do the job," he said abstractly. "It might come in handy."

I shrugged my shoulders. Walker tossed the weapon and ammunition into the bag.

There were a couple of scented candles on top of the dresser. They were the kind of decorative things that people lit to set the mood for a romantic evening. I got to my feet and swept them into the bag, then stopped quite suddenly.

"How fast are the zombies, Walker?" I asked. "Could we outrun them – if we had to?"

Walker wrenched his mouth from side to side like he was considering the question. He shrugged. "Maybe," he said, and then he took a long deep breath. "The ones I've seen move awkwardly," he added. "I can't really explain it except to compare them to folks who have maybe lost a leg in an accident and are learning to walk again with a prosthetic limb. Maybe that's not a good explanation – but it's the best I can come up with. The undead move, but it is awkward movement – like they don't really have full control of their bodies."

"Hey," Jed said suddenly, and his head appeared from within the built-in wardrobe. "Some of those guys with artificial limbs are fuckin' fast. Ever heard of the Special Olympics?"

Walker's expression didn't change. He nodded. "You're right," he said. "And maybe some of the undead are just as fast. I really don't know. All I know is what I've seen."

I thought back to the night before and remembered the tall figure in the grassy field I had shot. I recalled his jerky, spasmodic gait.

"You say you have seen them – up close? This isn't just based on something you overheard, or heard on the news?" I asked.

"I know it," Walker said darkly, and the sound of his voice lowered and became pained. "I saw my wife die," he said. "She got cornered in our living room. I couldn't get to her. They came through the door – maybe six or seven of them. She couldn't get away, and I couldn't get to her..."

There was a long moment of silence, and Walker began to tear up. He cuffed at his eyes brusquely.

"And you say they're like sharks, right?"

"Right."

I shook my head. "But I don't understand something." I frowned. "If a zombie bites a person, they become infected with the virus, right?"

Walker nodded. "Right. Once bitten, a person will turn within about thirty seconds."

"But they're also driven to a frenzy by blood, right?"

"Right. Just like sharks."

I screwed up my face and shook my head. "Then how do they survive long enough to turn in the first place?" I asked. "If a zombie bites a person, there is going to be blood. So why don't the zombies just tear the person to pieces? And if they did, then how is the virus spreading at all? The zombies should be tearing every victim limb from limb because of the blood."

Walker stared at me for a long moment, and then began to speak slowly and deliberately. "I go back to the sharks analogy," he said patiently. "Imagine a shark swimming into a pack of tuna. The shark snaps and savages at everything swimming past it. Some of the tuna are killed and eaten. Others are maimed and swim away to die. The blood in the water and the thrashing of the tuna attracts more sharks. More of the tuna are killed – but even more are maimed in the frenzy."

Walker clasped his hands together. "That's how the infection spreads. The danger is when one of the undead corners a group of people. Some will die, but most will be bitten and stagger away.... long enough to turn."

I leaned back against the bedroom wall. I nodded.

"Shit," Jed said softly, his voice made hushed by dread and some kind of gruesome awe.

"Shit," I agreed.

Walker wasn't finished. He shook his head. "Have you seen any of the undead up close?"

"No," I said. "We saw some attacks through the window of the safe house, but they were on the opposite side of the street. When we escaped from Forresterville, we were in a car – until I crashed it. All we saw were teaming hordes of running, panicked people."

"Well it's not like the movies," Walker said. "The undead I saw – the ones that killed my wife – didn't have their chests shot out, or their arms missing. And their faces weren't torn away. Not yet, anyhow. Maybe the virus will change, but the undead I saw were still very human-like. But their skin is dry. Dry as grey paper," he said, rubbing at his own face as he spoke. "Their eyes are sunken, their cheeks hollowed... but they're not the stuff of blood-soaked B grade horror flicks. They're more... more real than that."

We left the main bedroom, carrying the nylon bag with us, and went into the room that was filled with stored furniture.

Everything was covered with a heavy dust sheet. There were a couple of tables stacked on

126

top of each other, a couple of wardrobes, a desk, bookcase and several low chests of drawers. We worked quickly, opening drawers and doors. We found nothing of value apart from a couple of Stephen King paperbacks that were on a shelf of the bookcase between a collection of cooking and gardening books. It stuffed the paperbacks into the bag.

We ignored the bathroom – I had searched the medicine cabinet above the vanity the night before, after I had cleaned up the blood from Jed's tooth extraction.

We gathered in the kitchen and Jed paused to glance warily through the gap in the curtains, out at the back yard. He shook his head. "Nothing moving," he said.

I let out a long breath. "Okay, we've found probably everything that might be useful to us," I said.

Jed interrupted.

"What about the little shed?" he asked. "The one by the fence. Was there anything in there?"

"Not a lot," I said, recalling my hasty search in the dark. "A few gardening tools, some bags of potting dirt…"

"What about in the garage?"

"Tools."

"A car?"

"No. Not even a pushbike."

Jed didn't look surprised. "What about weapons?"

"You mean guns?"

"No, dipshit. I mean tools that we could use as weapons. Hammers – that kind of thing."

I felt my anger start to boil. I had gone out into that garage in the middle of a damned storm, in the dark, to find pliers, so he could have is tooth removed. Now he was interrogating me.

"Gee, Jed. I don't remember," my temper flared. I felt the heat rising under the collar of my shirt, and my self-control slipping. I snapped at him. "I went out there to try to save your ass," I reminded him. "For all I know, there might be hammers. Hell, there might be an entire gun cabinet filled with machine guns I missed. *Why don't you go out and take a look for yourself.*"

Jed bristled and his face turned ugly – but Walker stepped smoothly between us, his voice low and calm. He planted a hand in the middle of my chest and pushed me away, then did the same to Jed. He stood between us, and his eyes were dark and black.

"Enough of this shit," he said, without a hint of emotion in his voice. He was completely cool. "We've got enough to deal with, without you two trying to rip each other's throats out. You're brothers, for fuck's sake. Why don't you try acting like it?"

Jed thought that was bitterly ironic. He huffed and puffed for another minute in silence until the tension went out of his expression. But he stayed up on the balls of his feet, his big fists bunched.

"Now we need to decide what to do next. We need to come up with a plan – and that ain't going to happen until you two calm the fuck down." Walker looked long and hard at Jed.

Jed grunted. "I'm calm."

Walker turned on me. "I'm calm," I said.

But I wasn't.

We went back into the living room, and found Harrigan standing in the middle of the floor with my gun raised uncertainly. He looked agitated.

"Everything all right?" he asked quickly. "I heard raised voices." Walker's daughter was standing behind him, shielded by the weighty expanse of his heavy frame. "I... I thought maybe..."

I waved away his fear. "Relax, Clinton. Everything's okay. Jed and I were just having a brotherly discussion, and Mr Walker was offering his opinion."

"That's all it was? I... I thought..."

"That's all it was," I assured him. "There's nothing going on outside. We've been checking the windows while we searched the house."

I crossed the room and took the gun from Harrigan. The sudden storm of noise in the kitchen had really rattled him.

Slowly, the girl emerged from hiding. She went and stood beside her father, like she was glued to his hip.

I dropped down to the floor and rubbed at my face like it was frozen and I was trying to get the blood circulating. I was suddenly very tired. I felt it in my bones – the weary ache of exhaustion and nerves that had been strung taut for too long. The tension was getting to all of us – and I realized it wasn't likely to get any easier.

"We need to decide what we're going to do," I sighed, echoing Walker's comment in the kitchen. "We can't stay here forever, and we know help is unlikely to arrive. We're on our own, people. We've got to make the best of it."

One by one the others got comfortable on the floor around me. Only Harrigan stayed on his feet. He stood in the hallway entrance like he was unsure what to do – join the conversation, or keep watch through the kitchen window.

I waved him down. "This is important, Clinton. You should have a say. It's your life – and our lives – we're talking about. I don't want anyone to complain that they didn't have a chance to speak, once we reach a decision."

Harrigan stayed in the hallway opening, but reluctantly slid his back down the wall until he was sitting. But he wasn't at all relaxed. He looked like he was poised to spring to his feet at the slightest sound.

Half a minute passed in total silence, thirty seconds before I spoke. When at last, I did, my voice was flat and devoid of any emotion, a low monotone in the eerie hush that was broken only by the sound of breathing.

"This meeting isn't to decide if we should move from this house," I said. "It's to decide which way we go when we leave – and whether we should stay as a group, or separate."

I hadn't thought about that second option – hadn't thought about it at all until the instant the words slipped from my mouth. It caught me – and everyone else by surprise.

The silence in the room was a heavy melancholy gloom, the tension becoming more palpable. I saw Jed's eyes narrow into cunning, calculating little slits, and I saw Harrigan inhale a sudden sharp breath. Only Walker seemed not to react. It was like the man was carved from stone.

"Separating would be a bad idea," Walker said, and his voice dropped to a low rumble like distant thunder. He leaned forward, his face intent and serious. "There's strength in numbers. More guns – more eyes. There are enough of us for the group to rest while others guard. We will stand a better chance," he said. "If we separate, we will all die." Walker was worried all right – I could hear it in his voice – but he wasn't scared. In fact he didn't look like the kind of man that scared easily.

I saw Harrigan from the corner of my eye. He was nodding his head. I glanced at Jed. He glared back at me.

"That makes sense," I conceded. I remembered the terror of those first days of the apocalypse before Jed and I had stumbled upon the safe house. They were dark horrifying days and nights filled with nerve-wracking anxiety. There hadn't been a single moment to relax, or a moment to rest. It was a waking nightmare of constant fear that went on without end.

There were still problems that needed answers. My eyes made another searching sweep across the faces gathered around, and then I started with the biggest question of all. "Where do we go?"

Walker spoke immediately, which surprised me. I had formed the opinion that he was the kind of man who sat back and watched, and only intervened or became involved after carefully assessing a situation. But now his voice had a restrained measure of urgency to it.

"We head towards Pentelle," he said. Emphatic.

For several seconds the room remained silent. Finally it was Jed who spoke.

"Why?" he asked, his attitude petulant and simmering with rebellion. "Why not head towards Richmond? Or why don't we get onto the 64 and make a run towards West Virginia?" He got to his feet quite suddenly and stabbed his finger in Walker's direction but his question was aimed squarely at me and Harrigan. "Why are we just going where this guy wants us to go?"

"It's not where I want to go," Walker's calm restraint slipped a notch. "It's the only place left to go," he said. He came to his feet like a cat, surprisingly agile for a big man. Secretly, I guessed that Walker and Jed would be a good physical match for each other. Jed was an inch taller, and maybe a few pounds of muscle heavier, but Walker moved like he knew how to fight. He carried his strength in his shoulders and thighs, and looked like he was more than capable of trading blows in a fist-fight.

"Richmond is a slaughter-house. And West Virginia is a wasteland. There's nothing left, man," Walker said. "Life no longer exists the way it once did. There are only the undead, those about to become undead – and a few thousand survivors, aboard navy vessels in the Atlantic, east of Norfolk. There's nothing else," he said. "Nothing at all."

I turned to Harrigan. So far he hadn't said a word. "Clinton? You're part of this group. What do you think?"

For a long time Harrigan said nothing. There was no sound at all. Everyone's head turned towards him, and he got slowly to his feet, almost statesman-like, as though he were burdened with some dreadful news he was about to share.

His eyes swept across our faces, and then finally he said, "I vote that we attempt to reach Pentelle," he said slowly, "– but it won't make any difference. We're all going to die."

He didn't say it with his words filled with panic. He didn't say it with his face twisted in fear or despair. He said it like it was a simple, unavoidable statement of fact. That's what scared me.

I stared at him, stunned. "What?"

He slid his hand deep inside the pocket of his trousers and pulled out the small worn copy of his Bible. He had a page marked and the book fell open.

"And this shall be the plague wherewithin the Lord will smite all the people

That have fought against Jerusalem;

Their flesh shall consume away while they stand upon their feet,

And their eyes shall consume away in their holes,

And their tongue shall consume away in their mouth."

He closed the book, and tucked it back into his pocket. "That was Zechariah 14:12," Harrigan explained.

I didn't know what to say. None of us did. We all stared at Harrigan for half a minute, and he stared right back at us, his gaze level and steady. Even Jed seemed stunned to silence.

I frowned. "Then why vote for trying to reach Pentelle, Clinton?" I asked gently. "Why didn't you vote to stay here – to hide and wait it out? If you think the Bible has predicted doomsday, then why are you in favor of trying to travel forty miles through hordes of infected ghouls?"

Harrigan smiled – but it was a listless, tired gesture, like he had already considered the question himself, and already knew the answer. "Because," he said softly, "it's better to die on your feet than live on your knees. And if we're going to die – if the good Lord has turned His back on a world filled with sinners – then I want to die trying."

Harrigan sounded like a wise old prophet who had just come down from the mountaintop. It surprised me, but it shouldn't have. He was a thoughtful, intelligent man. He never said much, but I had learned during the last week that when he spoke, he was a man worth listening to.

I turned back to Jed. "Do you still vote in favor of heading to Richmond, or West Virginia?"

He glared at me and screwed up his face. "Is there any point?"

"No," I shook my head. "Not really. Not unless you want to go alone, because it seems that the rest of us are heading south – to Pentelle."

I looked back to Walker. "When?"

He looked a little bemused. "Why are you handing all these decisions to me?" he asked slowly. "Have you finally decided that I'm trustworthy?"

I smiled coldly. "No," I said. "But I'm trusting you to make the best decisions for your daughter's safety. You're the military guy, and you're the one who knows about the Jaws virus. You're the most likely one amongst us to make good choices."

He sat back down and thought for a moment. "If we go tonight, we would be travelling in the dark," he said. "We'd need to find a car and navigate our way through the suburbs until we could get onto the highway." He made a sound like he was sucking air through his teeth. "On the one hand, we have the cover of darkness, but on the other hand, we'll never see what's coming. We won't have time for alternative options."

"But surely the cover of dark is a big advantage," I said. "Especially if we can stay quiet."

"In a car?" Walker shook his head. "Any undead within a mile will be drawn by the sound of the engine. And remember, the cover of darkness only conceals us until we find a car. From the moment we gun the engine, we're going to become targets."

I sat back. "So it's daylight. Tomorrow."

"Walker nodded. "We'll be at risk from the moment we leave this house until the moment we find a car," he said. "But after that we'll have the advantage of daylight. If the road is blocked with wrecked debris, we might be able to go around. Once we make it to the freeway, the going will get easier." Then he shrugged, as if to say, *'well it's a plan, but it's not a very good plan'.*

I glanced over my shoulder at Harrigan. He nodded, but said nothing more. Jed huffed and blustered for a few seconds and then stormed out into the kitchen.

The discussion washed away into heavy silence. Harrigan disappeared down the hallway. I guess I became grim and reflective. In twenty-four hours we were going to burst out of the house and make a mad, desperate dash for a car – supposing we could find one before the undead filled the streets and we were torn to pieces. But I had no illusions that our escape would be the romantic stuff of movies. This wouldn't be a guns-blazing charge into legend – it was going to be a terrifying, stomach-churning scramble.

Harrigan was gone for some time, and when he finally came back into the living room, there was something in his face. Maybe frustration, or concern – I couldn't tell. He was carrying a couple of cans of soda. He handed me one without saying a word and offered the other to Walker. Walker shook his head curtly. Clearly, there were more important things on his mind. His face was pale and full of worry.

"Best-case scenario is that we find an SUV nearby," Walker said. "One with the keys in the ignition, and a full tank of gas."

I almost laughed, but feared if I did, I might sound slightly hysterical. "I don't like your chances," I said.

"No, neither do I," Walker admitted. "But even a mid-sized sedan will do until we can get clear to the freeway," he said. "Half a tank of gas would be enough. Once we're in the clear, we'll have time to look for a better option."

"Have you thought about a driver?" I asked.

He stared at me. "You."

"Me?" I was appalled. "My driving record isn't too good," I reminded him. "I crashed the first car Jed and I escaped in, and I killed the second one."

Walker seemed deaf. "You," he said again. "And your brother up front beside you."

I frowned at that. "Maybe Jed should be in the driver's seat…"

Walker shook his head. "No," he said. "At least you are mentally stable. I'm not so sure about your brother – and besides, he looks like he would enjoy the violence of blazing away at the undead. I'd hate to deny him the opportunity if it comes to that."

I shrugged. "So that puts you and Harrigan in the back seat."

"Yes. With Millie wedged in between us where she will be safest. Give Harrigan your Glock – you can't shoot and drive at the same time – but maybe carry the little revolver if you think you would feel better being armed."

"I would," I said meaningfully. "I most definitely would."

I cracked open the can of soda. It was blood-warm and tasted like drain cleaner.

* * *

Time crept by slowly. Daylight dragged on and on. I spent some time reading one of the Stephen

King books, and a lot more time sitting alone in the silence, wondering if this was what it was like for those who served in the military, counting down the hours until an attack. Was this what it was like for the heroes of D-Day during World War II? Were those men nervous and trembling in the hours before boarding the massed invasion craft that swept across the English Channel? Were they so scared they felt physically ill?

What about Jed and Harrigan? Were they feeling the same nauseating, debilitating fear that clawed at me?

And what about Colin Walker? He said he was ex-military. I wondered if he had served at the pointy end of the spear in the Middle East, and whether fear was a shadowy companion for all of us.

Or was it just me?

We took turns on guard duty at the kitchen window, while the others slept. Not that there seemed to be a lot of sleeping going on. The floor was hard and uncomfortable. After an hour of tossing, I crept out to the kitchen and relieved Harrigan who was standing watch. I stole a quick glance through the curtains. The sun was setting. Harrigan and I exchanged a few desultory words, but there wasn't much to say. He drifted down the hallway and I took another can of soda from the pantry and sipped at it while my thoughts swirled round in ever-decreasing circles of fear and death.

I suddenly heard soft footsteps behind me and I whirled on the spot. Walker's daughter, Millie, was standing in the kitchen doorway. She had slipped off her shoes and was creeping through to the bathroom.

She froze, and her eyes went wide. I saw her clutch instinctively for the bracelet on her wrist and wrap her fingers round the chunky floral detail.

"Hi," I said softly.

The girl said nothing.

"Millie, right? My name is Mitch. Mitch Logan. We haven't had a chance to talk since the helicopter accident."

The girl said nothing. She stood perfectly still, like a forest animal on the edge of a clearing – ready to flee at the first sign of danger.

I had the Glock in my hand. I set it down on the kitchen cupboard and offered her the can of soda. Her eyes searched my face – and then she reached out and took the can from me.

"It tastes like warm piss," I said. The girl blinked.

I apologized.

She sipped at the drink, then handed it back.

"You're fifteen, right?"

She nodded.

"I'm sorry about your mother. Your dad said she died in the first days of the outbreak."

The girl frowned, like she was annoyed. Maybe she thought such personal matters weren't to be shared with strangers. Maybe she had a sudden memory of her mother before the apocalypse. She bit her lip, and then said softly, "That's right."

"And you don't have any brothers or sisters who might have escaped? There's just you and your dad?"

She nodded. "I'm an only child."

I made a wry face. "I wish I was…"

The girl said nothing.

I leaned back against the kitchen counter. The girl still hadn't moved. "Do you remember much of what happened when the helicopter went down?"

The girl shook her head. "No," she said. "Just a lot of noise and smoke."

I nodded. "You and your dad were lucky to survive."

Millie didn't look so sure about that. She stared at me for long seconds, with an expression that seemed almost a glare of defiance, then her demeanor altered and she shrugged her shoulders. "I guess so."

"It is a pity about the pilot… did you know him?"

"No," she shook her head again, and the long tresses of her hair flicked across her shoulders like a swishing tail.

I studied her face very carefully. There was no doubt that the helicopter crash and our subsequent close escape from the undead had terrified this girl. I had seen her face – seen the look of sheer horror in her eyes. They were looks that couldn't be faked – not by a fifteen year old kid. She had been scared out of her mind.

But now…?

I wasn't getting the sense that this girl was so traumatized – so deeply scarred – that she could barely put two words together without collapsing in a blubbering mess of tears and trembling. Not at all.

In fact, now I was getting the impression that this girl wasn't frightened at all any more. She was guarded. Wary.

Maybe her father had given her the mother of all *'don't talk to strangers'* speeches.

She crept past me to the bathroom without another word, and I turned back to the window. She was gone for a few minutes. I heard her footsteps as she passed back through the kitchen, but I didn't turn around. I kept staring out through the window.

I was thinking troubled thoughts.

Chapter Four.

Sunrise.

I stayed awake through the night and watched the morning dawn bright and clear and blue through the kitchen curtains. My eyes felt gritty and raw. When I heard the stirring, shuffling sounds of people waking, I went down the hallway towards the living room.

The room looked like the aftermath of a plane crash. Millie was curled up on the sofa chair with her head tilted back towards the ceiling, and her legs tucked uncomfortably beneath her bottom. Harrigan and Jed were lying sprawled across the floor. Jed was on his back, one arm flung wide and the other across his face, as though shielding his eyes from the light. Harrigan was lying on his side. He was awake. I saw him gazing up at me with an expressionless face. I looked him in the eye for a couple of seconds then turned away.

Walker was half-laying and half-sitting, his body resting up against the side of the sofa, and his legs thrust straight out in front of him. His body was limp, like a wounded man who had been propped up until the paramedics could attend to him. But he wasn't asleep. His breathing was deep and steady and rhythmic, and yet I noticed the flickering movement of his eyes behind the closed lids. I stood perfectly still and watched him until he went through the pantomime of waking – complete with a convincing yawn and tight-muscled stretch of his arms. His eyes went straight to mine. They were clear and alert. He knew I had been watching him, and I guessed he knew that I knew he had been awake all along. But neither of us said anything.

"I thought you army ninja types slept with your eyes open, Mr Walker."

The corner of his mouth twisted up. It could have been a smile – but it might have been a grimace. He said nothing. He got to his feet, and the movement stirred his daughter awake. She blinked and yawned, still muzzy with sleep, until a moment later when the realization of where she was struck her like a delayed shock. She looked up at me.

"Morning," I said.

The girl looked towards her father, as if she should take her cue from him, but Walker had crossed to the full-length window. He had his back to us.

"Morning," she said softly, then looked quickly away.

I got the message.

I went down on my haunches beside Harrigan. "I know you slept well," I said, trying to sound upbeat. "You've got a body like a mattress – all that soft padding. Must be like sleeping on a cloud."

Harrigan grunted and rolled onto his back. "A man who loves and trusts the Lord as his Savior always sleeps well, Mitch" he said – and I wasn't sure if he was serious, or mocking me.

Breakfast was silent and tense. Even though the morning had dawned clear, the gloom as we huddled over cans of beans and the last of the sodas was like a heavy cloud. Hardly anybody spoke. Millie ate nothing at all, and even Harrigan picked at the contents of his can like a sparrow.

As we sat, Walker went through the process of stripping each of our guns, checking them meticulously, and reloading each weapon. Jed had a spare magazine for his Glock, and Walker had one for his own weapon. He emptied them of ammunition, and then reloaded each of them. Finally, he emptied the shells from the little revolver and slid in fresh ones. He handed it to me without a word.

Everyone was looking at me, waiting for me to speak; sitting in a tight semi circle around the candle, even though it had long since been extinguished. The only sound in the room was the sound of Jed, eating with gluttonous ignorance, mouth open as he chewed, and thick sauce dribbling down the coarse dark stubble of his chin.

I sighed to myself.

My mouth was dry, and sweat was breaking out in the palms of my fists.

In the era of Napoleon, the British army had a peculiar tradition prior to engaging an enemy that was behind a fortified defense. The army called for volunteers to storm the ramparts, knowing that the first attack was likely to be a desperate, suicidal assault. They called the men the 'forlorn hope'. I looked at the faces around me and wondered whether the wretched thing we were about to do would end in the same monstrous bloodshed – with the same tragic results.

"When we get outside, we stay together – no matter what," I said, looking pointedly in the direction of my brother. "We move as a group."

Walker nodded. "That's right," he said. "No one goes off alone. We look for a car and we do it moving in a tight knot, with every gun covering every angle."

The nylon bag was heavier now, weighed down with the ransacked supplies we had gathered from searching the house. I zipped it shut, and slid it across to Jed. "It's your responsibility," I said. "You're big enough to lug it, and not be slowed down. If I put that thing on my back I'll buckle at the knees."

Jed's face soured suspiciously. "Let Harrigan carry it," he said. "Or G.I. Joe, here. Why has it gotta be me?"

I sighed again. "Because Harrigan is going to be watching the girl, and Walker is going to be taking the lead," I said patiently. "You're the only choice – unless you're prepared to put your life on the line, if need be, to keep the girl safe."

Jed thought about that – for less than a second. He nodded and dragged the bag towards him. He got to his feet and tested the weight of it slung over his shoulders, looking at me defiantly as though the bag weighed nothing at all.

The gesture reminded me once again why my brother was so dangerous; he was a dumb, ignorant, selfish brute. Jed was a thug. It was as simple as that. I could trust him – but only to do what was in his own best interests. As long as our efforts served his purpose, he would be a reluctant part of the group.

But not for a single moment longer.

Once the group outlived its usefulness, I knew that I too would have outlived his need for me. That would be the moment he would seek his revenge.

That would be the moment he would kill me.

We all got to our feet and drifted towards the front door, like a group of skydivers about to leap from a plane – without parachutes. I pulled on my leather jacket, and helped Harrigan shrug on his heavy coat. He had my Glock in one meaty fist and his crow-bar in the other. We exchanged a silent look, and then I wrapped my hand around the cold brass knob of the handle and took a long deep breath.

Walker stood right behind me, with Millie pressed at his side. Walker checked his weapon one last time, and I heard Jed and Harrigan do the same.

"It's now, or never," I said, the words like jagged glass in the back of my throat. I unlocked the door – and pulled it slowly open.

* * *

I went out the door and onto the porch, squinting into the bright glare of morning sunlight and feeling the slap of fresh warm air on my face. My heart was racing like a trip-hammer in my chest, and the sound of blood fizzing in my ears was almost deafening. I had the little revolver in my hand, arm extended, and I swept the barrel of the weapon in an arc that covered the lush green grass across the front lawn.

Nothing. I felt Walker's bulky shape pressed against my side but I didn't look at him. I heard the others, but my eyes stayed fixed and searching. There was no movement, no sound – not even the sound of birds or breeze.

Dead silence.

I hesitated for a split-second. I honestly don't know what I had expected as I burst out through the doorway, but it wasn't this. My nerves were drawn tight as a bow. I could feel the trembling tension in my thighs and arms.

I stole a glance at Walker. His face was grim, his mouth a thin line.

"Go!" he whispered, the single word inflected with anxiety and fear and urgency. "And don't look back." He shoved the flat of his hand between my shoulder blades.

I went.

I went at a run, leaping down from the low veranda and landing in the long grass. I could feel nervous sweat blistering across my brow and trickling down my back. After the heavy rains, the air was thick and humid. Sweat stung my eyes. My head twisted and turned, never still for a moment, and the pistol bounced and wavered with the jolt of every step.

I went left, through a low garden of bright yellow flowers, and glanced at the house up ahead.

It was a single story brick home, with a big bay window beneath an aluminum awning. The window had been broken, the frame twisted and mangled. I saw blood on the curtains and more blood on the window sill. I kept running.

There was a paved driveway on the opposite side of the house with a median strip of grass. I ran towards it. I could hear the scrabble of heavy pounding footsteps close behind me. I could feel Walker's presence, seeming to hang over my shoulder like the shadow of death. I could hear ragged breathing and Harrigan grunting with the effort of keeping up with the group.

I reached the corner of the house and snapped a glance left. The driveway was empty. Where the pavers abruptly ended was a high wrought iron gate, and behind it a garage door.

I started to slow…

"No!" Walker breathed heavily, as though he could read my mind. "Keep going."

I didn't argue. I ran on towards the next house. The street was gradually curving, and as I rounded the gentle bend I saw a burned out car in the middle of the road. The car was sitting down on its steel rims. The tires had melted away. The windshield and side windows were all gone and the paintwork had been vaporized so all that remained of the sheet metal was scorched grey. The blacktop was bubbling, and tendrils of wispy smoke still drifted up into the morning sky.

There was a charred body beside the vehicle with a crow perched on its back, pecking at the remains. I couldn't tell if the body was a man or a woman. The hair had been singed away and all that was left of the corpse were disfigured blackened lumps.

I looked up. The next house on the block was another single story brick home with a steeply angled roof, like maybe the owners had renovated and built extra space into the attic. There was a silver sedan on the front lawn, grass growing up around the tires, and a red station wagon parked in the driveway.

"Yes!" I heard Walker hiss, and his voice rose with triumph and relief. "Try the station wagon first."

I veered towards the driveway. The wagon was a Honda Crosstour – maybe only twelve months old. The duco sparkled in the sunlight.

I went to the driver-side and snatched at the door handle. It was locked. I pressed my face hard against the window. I couldn't see any keys in the ignition.

"Try the other doors!" Walker hissed at me. He went down into a crouch, his back pressed against the car, his gun swinging in an arc to cover the street.

Harrigan went to the other side of the car, and we tried every door. They were all locked.

"I'll smash the fuckin' window!" Jed snarled. He raised the butt of the Glock to use it like a hammer, but Walker snatched at his wrist.

"Forget it!" Walker hissed. "No noise. We'll try the sedan."

We moved in a tight knot towards the car parked on the front lawn. It was an old and tired Ford Taurus that looked like it had endured two decades of hard driving. The paintwork was dull, the windshield covered with a layer of dirt and grime. There were ugly scars of rust on the front fenders. The passenger side window had been lowered half an inch – maybe to let the heat out as the car sat baking under the summer sun. I tried the door. It was locked. I thrust my fingers into the gap between the window and pulled down hard. The glass moved a quarter of an inch, and then stopped.

"Here!" I heard Harrigan hiss. He was on the other side of the Taurus. He had the driver's door open. He clambered into the car and reached across to unlock the doors.

I pulled open the door I was standing by and stole a glance around me. Walker was kneeling against the front fender, gun arm extended, covering the street. Jed was right behind Harrigan, with his gun arm extended towards the nature strip on the far side of the road. Walker's daughter was standing behind me like a shadow. She was jigging with terror from foot to foot, the tension and simmering panic raw in her expression.

"Keys?" Walker hissed over his shoulder, never taking his eyes from the street.

"No," Harrigan hissed. "Wait a minute."

He pulled down the car's sun visors. Nothing. He thrust his hands under the driver's seat and then ransacked the cracked faded plastic pockets and crevices of the car's console.

"We don't have a minute!" Walker spat.

Harigan backed out of the car empty handed. Jed swore bitterly under his breath. "Want me to wire it?"

"Can you?" Walker called back at him.

"Give me a minute."

"We don't have a fucking minute!" Walker said again. I felt the panic in me rising. We were totally exposed – totally vulnerable, standing by the side of the road, clustered around a car in the blazing morning light.

"Fuck it!" Walker spat venomously. "There's another car in the middle of the road about fifty yards away," he fumed with frustration. "We're going for it."

We left the Taurus with its doors wide open and moved quickly towards the abandoned car. I felt Walker's daughter clutch at my hand as we ran. Her grip was fierce, her finger nails digging into the flesh of my palm. Walker was in the lead. He went forward at a run, and Jed was beside him, their footsteps sounding loud as pounding hooves. Harrigan ran alongside the girl and me, but we couldn't keep pace. Walker and Jed reached the car ten yards ahead of us.

It was a blue Japanese sedan, left skewed across the blacktop. The driver's door was open, and there was a body hanging out through the door. I saw a woman's legs in high-heel shoes. Jed leaned into the car and grabbed hold of the body. He dragged the woman's limp shape out onto the road. She was decomposing.

I reached the car. Jed's face was wrenched into a fierce, berserker's expression. His eyes were wild, every fiber in his body singing with adrenalin. He threw himself into the driver's seat. He was breathing hard, mouth wide open. He stomped his foot on the gas and pumped the pedal. There were keys in the ignition. I stood there, gasping, and held my breath. The engine whirred then died. Jed thumped the wheel with his fist.

Walker was on the passenger side of the car. He pulled the door open and then reached through to unlock the rear door.

"As soon as this thing kicks over, pile in!"

Jed tried the engine again. It whirred and died again. I heard him spit a tirade of abuse at the car, and then a flicker of movement caught the corner of my eye.

I turned my head towards a clapboard house directly opposite the car. It was a worn old building, paint flaking from the walls and the roof tiles stained and moss-covered. There was a big curtained window facing the street. I narrowed my eyes.

The curtains twitched. I stared, feeling a chill of apprehension blow down my spine. My breath jammed in my throat.

My first impulse was to shout a warning, but I crushed down on the urge and forced myself to disentangle my hand from the girl's. I glanced further along the street, then back to the window. There was a dark shadowed shape behind the curtains – a shape like a head. It was moving – rocking from side to side.

I felt my skin prickle, like a thousand insects were crawling over my body. I turned to the girl and grabbed her shoulders fiercely. "Stay here," I said in an urgent whisper. "Do not move. Understand?" The girl nodded her head with jerky confusion, but then clawed for my hand. I caught her wrist. "Stay here!" I hissed.

I went around the trunk of the car, and put my hand on Walker's shoulder. He whirled round, his eyes fierce and frantic.

"The clapboard house," I said, looking Walker in the eye. "There's someone – or something – at the front window." Somehow I managed to keep my voice low and calm, even though my stomach was churning with swollen knots of fear.

Walker was good. I knew the urge for him to turn his head and stare at the window would have been almost impossible to resist, but resist he did. He nodded at me and actually looked away – further along the street.

"Are you sure?"

"Yeah," I said. "There's something there."

"Just one?"

I shook my head. "I don't know – but if we don't get this car running in the next few seconds, we're going to be in a world of pain out here in the middle of the road."

Walker nodded. "Get back around the other side of the car," he said. "Make sure Millie is covered, and let Harrigan know what's going on. If they come from that house, I'm going to need you to cover me."

He ducked his head through the passenger door and spoke briefly to Jed. I heard the engine suddenly whine again – a tired, weary sound – and then more muttered curses.

I got back around the car and prodded Harrigan in the back. He was leaning against the rear door, with my Glock in his hand, covering the scrubby fringe of nature strip. Millie was standing close beside him, dwarfed by his enormous bulk and size.

"They're in the house on the other side of the road," I said quietly. "Clapboard house. There is a window at the front. I saw movement there. Might be one – might be a thousand."

Harrigan didn't have the training or discipline of Walker. The big man's head turned like it was on rusty hinges and he gaped at the building, then back at me.

"You sure?"

"Yes," I said.

"Then why aren't they attacking?"

I shook my head. "Maybe we're not making enough noise to set them off," I shrugged. "Maybe the noise isn't distinct enough."

Millie made a strangled sound of alarm – a whimper of panic in the back of her throat. I pulled the back door open and held it. Jed was in the front seat, hunched over the wheel. I could see the back of his head, and the tense cords of muscles in his neck. He tried to start the car again, hissing abuse under his breath as the engine whirred then died again.

"Sit on the back seat," I told Millie. "Right behind Jed. If we get the car started, you will be safe. We will all pile in around you."

She sat on the back seat, sidesaddle, with her feet hanging out of the car and her bottom perched on the edge of the upholstery. I leaned over the roof of the car, resting my gun arm on the hot sun baked metal with my knees rubbing against the rear tire.

Walker ducked back through the passenger door and I heard the raw tension in his voice as he struggled to keep his words to a whisper.

"Has it got fuel?"

"Half a fuckin' tank!" I heard Jed hiss.

"Then try it again."

The engine groaned, and I felt the car rock on its hinges, as though Jed was desperately trying to urge the car into life. Then suddenly the engine coughed – and died.

"Again!" Walker hissed.

The motor spluttered, gasped – and then burst into reluctant life, like an old man coming awake. For brief seconds the beat of the motor was fragile and uncertain, and then quite suddenly it wailed into a full-throated roar of smoke and noise.

I heard Jed give a ragged cheer of expletive-filled relief. He sawed his foot up and down the gas pedal until the motor was revving high and hard.

"Get in!" Walker screamed.

This wasn't the plan – but then no plan was ever perfect.

Jed was in the driver's seat and Walker in the passenger seat. I ran around to the other side of the car and threw myself through the door so Millie was jammed between me and Harrigan's comforting man-mountain of bulk. The interior of the car smelled like leaked gasoline and rotting food. My door was still swinging open. I reached out for it – at the same instant the front window of the house exploded outwards in a shattering blast of flying glass.

155

A chair landed on the front lawn, and then the figure of a man hurled itself through the jagged opening. He was hideous. His skin was grey and drawn like the withered skin of an onion. He was a tall shape. He landed on his feet, and came lurching towards me, dragging one of its legs behind it.

"Go! Go! Go!" I shouted. I heaved the car door shut. Walker's window in the front of the car was down. I saw him jam his gun out through the opening and pull the trigger.

The sound slammed painfully into my eardrums, and the recoil threw Walker's hand high. The undead lurching shape on the roadside staggered drunkenly, and then toppled into the grass.

I felt my body thrown back hard against the seat and there was a scream of squealing tires. The car filled with the stench of blue smoke and burning rubber and we were catapulted forward, weaving across the blacktop as Jed fought to get control of the wheel.

I heard Millie scream. Her body was twisted, her head wrenched round, staring out through the rear window. The ghoul was getting back to its feet, rising up from the ground but dwindling in the distance as the car surged forward.

"Oh, Jesus no!"

The despairing tone – not the words – made me snap my head around. It had been Jed's voice, flat and strangled of all life. A voice that sounded dead and desolate.

I stared forward through the windshield, between the broad shapes of Jed and Walker's bodies. The whole road ahead was filling with dark figures that spilled from the neighboring houses, the rustling keening sound in their throats an undulating hypnotic chant that crackled in the air like electricity.

There was at least a hundred of them, drawn inexorably by the noise of the revving engine, shambling and staggering and convulsing in a broken tide of bodies that surged towards us.

"Turn around!" I heard Walker bark.

"There's no room!" Jed snapped back. It was a typical suburban street. By the time he spun the car around in a three-point turn, the undead would be swarming all over us.

"Then speed up!"

"What?"

"Hit the gas!"

Jed crushed his foot down on the pedal and the sedan leaped forward. The space between the undead and us telescoped – reduced to nothing in an instant.

"Wind your windows up!" Walker shouted a warning – and then he reached across the car and reefed down hard on the steering wheel.

He caught Jed by surprise. The car swerved on tired spongy springs, and rolled like a big boat. We were veering towards the curb.

"Keep going!" Walker shouted.

"You're a crazy bastard!" Jed shouted back. "Hang on!"

The car mounted the curb with a bone-jarring crack that hurled us forward in our seats. I felt my head smash against something hard, and my vision shattered into a million shards of dazzling light. I tasted the warm coppery tang of blood in my mouth, and then everyone was screaming and shouting in panicked fear.

I shook my head. We were bumping and jolting across someone's lawn, the car's tires churning up clods of muddy earth and flinging them high into the air. Jed was tugging at the wheel like he was wrestling a grizzly bear. We crashed through a bushy green fern and then the car fishtailed into the side of a low brick fence, but kept going. The sound of groaning grinding metal was a noise like the dying shriek of some terrible beast.

There were half-a-dozen undead ahead of us. Their dark wretched shapes filled the windshield. The car ploughed into them and flung their bodies across the hood. I saw the figure of a woman bounced off the driver-side fender. She spun in a tight circle and then slammed into a power pole. Another of the undead disappeared under the front wheels. The car jolted and leaped and the engine screamed and strained.

I clung to the seat with grim terror. Millie was sobbing. The car spun wildly then crashed through a mailbox and landed back onto the blacktop. Harrigan's big body swayed and lurched from side to side, crushing the girl between us. Arms and legs went everywhere and the sound of our cries and panicked screams reached a terrifying crescendo. Then the tires caught traction in a howl of rubber and smoke, and we were suddenly skidding out of control towards the opposite side of the road.

I saw Jed wrench the wheel. He was hunched deep in the driver's seat, huge muscled forearms braced and his face rigid and grim. He caught the skid at the last possible moment. The car jounced up onto two wheels for an instant and then righted itself with a sickening thud and a mournful groan of metal.

We were through the undead.

There was only clear road ahead.

We sped towards safety. Relief washed over me like a wave.

And then two gunshots rang out – clear and piercingly loud, the sound of their retort echoing in the morning sky.

The car lurched – dropped down on one side – and slewed out of control.

"Jesus!" Jed shouted, and the raw fear in his voice frightened me even more than the sound of the gunshots. He slammed on the brakes and turned the wheel violently. The sudden change in the car's inert weight was catastrophic. I felt the car gouge down on the passenger side, and then we were veering out of control.

"Look out!" I heard Walker shout. The car hung over on two wheels and then miraculously righted itself, only to plough head-on into the back of a flat-bed truck left abandoned on the side of the road.

The impact was like a mighty fist being slammed into the center of my chest. I felt my head snapped forward and for an instant I was weightless. The sound of crushing rending metal was like the blast of an explosion in my ears. Everything went black, then the world came swimming back into focus through dust and thick swirling smoke.

There was a stunned silence that lasted long seconds. We had covered less than a couple of miles. The undead were out of sight, but I wondered for how long.

I had lost my gun, and as I threw my weight against the crumpled door, I groped for it. I caught a glimpse of Millie's terrified face. She was huddled down in the seat, and there was a thin razor-like gash on her forehead welling fat round droplets of blood.

"Are you all right?"

She groaned. Her hand went to her head in slow motion and when her fingers pressed against the wound she winced painfully. I glanced past her. Harrigan was slumped heavily in the corner of the seat, eyes closed, mouth agape. I reached past the girl and shook the big man hard. He groaned, and came awake like a boxer on the canvas struggling to beat the ten count.

"Are you okay?"

Harrigan groaned again. He sighed deeply and his eyes fluttered open, dull and unfocussed. I forgot about him and hurled my weight against the door.

The air was thick with swirling tendrils of smoke, and the smell of gas was strong and getting stronger. The door creaked open and I had to use my foot to pry it the rest of the way.

I got out of the car and staggered on unsteady feet. Everything seemed to spin and swirl around me. I clutched dizzily for the side of the sedan, and at that moment a gun opened fire. Bullets flailed the air around me, rattling and clanging against the car, tearing up fragments of stone and dirt and glass, ricocheting off into the distance. I ducked my head, made my body as small as I could and staggered to the sheltered side of the car.

Harrigan's face was pressed against the window of his door. I heaved against the handle, and the door flung open so unexpectedly that I lost my balance and fell backwards onto the sidewalk. Harrigan's heavy body fell out of the car and he lay crumpled and groaning in the gutter. I crawled to him.

"Come on, Clinton," I said through clenched teeth. "I need you, man!"

He staggered to his knees. I could see no obvious signs of injury – but I'm no doctor. The Glock was in the foot well behind the driver's seat. I lunged for it and thrust it into his big fist.

"There's someone shooting at us from one of the houses across the road," I said, almost shouting the words in his face to make them register through the haze of his disorientation. "I need you to cover me while I help the others."

Harrigan nodded, then glanced back down the street in the direction we had come. Nothing moved – yet.

I helped him to his feet and he slumped over the car, holding the gun in two hands and resting his arms on the crumpled metal roof. He seemed a little clearer – a little more steady. I reached across the seat and caught Millie's arm. She was tucked up in a trembling ball, knees under her chin, her hands covering her face. She was sobbing. I didn't have time for niceties. I grabbed her arm and heaved. I felt something tear in my chest and a flash of pain that exploded through the top of my head. I dragged the girl out of the car and pressed her down flat on the grass.

"Stay there!" I hissed at her. "Don't move!"

I heard more shots ring out. One smacked into the car. I didn't look up. I went to the driver's door and peered through the window at my brother.

Jed's head was slumped over the steering wheel. The whole front of the car had folded in, driving the engine block and the dashboard into his body. I heaved on the door but it wouldn't open. I tried again, straining with all my strength until I saw pinwheels of light burst into bright stars behind my eyes. The door had crumpled into the front wheel. I couldn't move it.

I climbed onto the back seat and reached around, groping for the driver's seat controls. There were a couple of plastic levers. I lifted the first one with my fingers but nothing happened. I tried the other one, and the backrest of the seat fell down towards me. Jed groaned.

I lowered the seat as far as I could. Jed rolled his head from side to side. I reached in and wrapped my arms around his chest. As I started to heave him backwards, he let out a fierce cry of pain.

I relaxed my grip and thrust my head through between the front seats. The front of the car was unrecognizable; a terrible mangled contortion of metal and plastic. I leaned over Jed and shoved my face close to his.

"Are your legs trapped?"

He groaned.

"Jed!"

He blinked his eyes open dazedly, and then winced in agony. I saw his eyes come into focus, hard and dark, but shadowed with pain. He spat blood down his chin and then wiped his mouth with the back of his hand.

"Can you feel your legs?" I barked urgently.

He nodded. I clambered back behind his seat and linked my hands under his armpits again. "Then if this hurts – too bad," I said.

I heaved. Jed cried out, but I ignored him. He slid back a couple of inches. I heaved again, turning him as I did so that I could drag him out of the car through the back seat. He came out in an awkward tangle of screaming pain. I stretched him out on the grass but he sat upright immediately.

"What the fuck…?"

I crouched over him.

"Someone shot out a tire," I spat. "They're in one of the houses across the street."

He shook his head and ran his tongue around the inside of his mouth like he was checking that he still had his teeth. "Zombies?"

"Zombies can't fire guns, dip-shit!" I said.

Jed grunted. "Walker?"

"I'm going for him now," I said. "Harrigan is keeping us covered."

Jed looked pained again. He pushed himself to his feet and balanced tenderly, like maybe one of his legs was broken. "Where's my gun?"

I gave him the revolver. He leaned himself over the roof of the car beside Harrigan.

I clambered back into the mangled wreckage of the car. Colin Walker was slumped against the backrest of his seat, his head turned to the side so that I could see his face was a mask of blood. The windshield had blown in on impact. There were thousands of tiny glittering pieces of glass across the man's lap and in his hair, and across his bloodied chest. I snatched at his wrist. His pulse was weak and racing erratically. He didn't move.

I left him and backed out of the car.

"Walker's not good," I said to Harrigan and Jed. I saw Millie's head snap round and her mouth fell open into a silent scream. I ignored her.

"I'm going to have to get him out through his door," I said grimly. "You'll have to cover me."

Harrigan shook his head. "You won't be able to do it on your own," he said. He stared at me. His eyes seemed clear. "I'm coming with you."

He gave the Glock to Jed and we hunched down together by the trunk of car.

"Ready?"

Harrigan nodded.

I jumped to my feet and ran around the side of the car. I heard myself screaming, and felt a sudden disruption of air around me that fanned my face like a hot dry wind as a bullet ricocheted off nearby wreckage. My heart was racing, fear knotting the strings of my nerves. I reached the passenger door and Harrigan was close behind me. I heard the loud *'blam'* of a gunshot and realized that Jed had returned fire.

I snatched at the car door and heaved. It didn't budge. Harrigan shouldered me aside and hurled his weight against the door. It came open with a rending groan. I ducked in through the door and at that instant the sound of the fire fight seemed to fade into the background.

Walker had been thrown forward by the collision at the same instant the windshield had exploded in on him. There was a wicked gash right across his forehead, and a wet livid slab of flesh hung down from his scalp across his eyes. Blood was spattered over his chest and in his lap. I backed out through the door, crouching down to make myself as small a target as possible for the hidden sniper, and tried to shut out the terrifying sounds of passing shots.

"Grab him," I said to Harrigan.

The big man reached in through the door and took hold of Walker's arms. When he was half out of the car, I scooped up his leaden legs and between us we carried him back behind the shelter of the wreckage. Jed fired two more shots and then ducked down behind the car.

"The fucker is in the brick two-story place," Jed hissed. He had his back against the car. He ran his eye over the stretched out body of Colin Walker and his expression became somber.

"He don't look too good."

I shook my head. I ripped open Walker's shirt and tore it into long strips. I pressed the loose flap of skin back against his forehead and bandaged it in place. His hair was matted thick with blood, and his face was pale, his lips turning a soft shade of blue.

Harrigan dropped to the grass beside Walker's prone body. The big man's hands were shaking. For that matter, so were mine.

He glanced over his shoulder, back along the empty street. I followed the direction of his gaze. The morning was hot, the land baking under a fierce summer sky. A heat haze rippled and shimmered off the blacktop. The road was empty – but the haunting sound of the undead we had driven through seemed to hang in the distant air.

"They're coming after us," Harrigan said, his voice flat and devoid of emotion. "Can't see 'em, but I can hear 'em."

I could too. We all could – the noise ebbing and drifting like a pulse.

Jed got up onto his haunches and narrowed his eyes in quick calculation. He pointed.

The nature strip on this side of the street had been left behind and we were in a built up area with houses on both sides of the road. The flat-bed truck had been parked out front of a single story brick home, and I glanced over my shoulder at it.

"We could get inside that house before they come," he said. "That only leaves the redneck with the AK to worry about."

I thought about it. Walker was in bad shape. I didn't think we could move him far. The undead were still out of sight, but not for much longer. If they crested the little undulating rise in the road and saw us, we were as good as dead.

I nodded. "Check it out," I said.

Jed went at a running crouch, using the wrecked car to cover him from the sniper across the street. I watched him all the way to the front porch of the house, weaving as he went, while the air around him snapped with the roar of gunfire. I turned back and leaned over Colin Walker.

"We're going to move you soon," I said. "We don't have much time. I'm afraid it's going to hurt, but there's nothing I can do about it. If we don't move soon, we'll die right here."

Walker said nothing. His chest heaved, labored and shallow, and the breath in his throat bubbled and gurgled. I cast another anxious glance down the length of the street, and then back to the front of the house where I had last seen Jed. The door was open, swinging ajar. I saw Jed's head and shoulders appear in the opening. He was smiling. He came back across the lawn, running awkwardly, bent-over at the waist.

"It's clear," he said. He was panting and wincing against some sharp pain. He had one big hand wrapped across his chest like he was holding in a shirt full of broken ribs. "No bodies. No bad guys. No dead guys."

I decided. "Okay. Let's do it."

But it wasn't that simple.

Walker couldn't be carried safely without anyone helping him standing upright and moving with his body slung between them. That meant exposing themselves to long dangerous seconds of fire. Even moving hunched in a bent-over crouch was risky. Sooner or later the gunman in the house opposite was going to get lucky.

"Grab the bag," I snapped at Harrigan.

I had stuffed a blanket inside the nylon bag before we had left the safe house. Now I unfolded it and spread it out on the patch of lawn sheltered from sight by the car wreck. "We'll get him on the blanket and drag him across the grass," I explained. It wasn't the best idea in the world –

but it would be faster than two men trying to carry him.

We sat Walker upright and slid the blanket beneath his back, but when I tried to lay him down again, he clutched fiercely at my shoulder – his grip so intense that it startled me. His eyes came wide open – clear as a mountain lake – and he stared at me with cold intent.

"Leave me," he said. "Give me a gun. I'll hold them off. You've got to get away from here. You've got to get Jessica to Pentelle. Nothing else matters." A froth of bloody bubbles appeared at the corner of his mouth and he gave a great weary sigh.

"*Jessica?* You mean Millie, your daughter…"

Walker shook his head, swallowed hard like he was trying to choke down jagged glass. "She's Jessica Steinman," he said. "She's not my kid. She's Jessica Steinman – the Vice President's daughter."

Nobody spoke.

Everyone was too stunned, too incredulous, trying to make sense of Walker's shocking revelation so that the silence stretched out for long numbed seconds. Gradually, slowly, we all turned our heads to look at the terrified teenage girl, seeing her now in a different light entirely.

I blinked. I shook my head – and stared at the girl while pieces of the puzzle I had worried over since the helicopter crash tumbled silently into place.

I frowned. "Is it true?"

The girl nodded. "I'm Jessica Steinman," she said. Her voice was shaky, choked, I suppose, with

168

a myriad of emotions at that moment. "Mr Walker is my bodyguard. He's Secret Service."

My eyes drifted to Harrigan. His face was blank and staring with astonishment. Then suddenly he twisted his head over his shoulder, like he had heard a new noise. He turned slowly back to me, and his face was drawn tight with alarm, his eyes wide and ominous.

I heard it too: the sound of thumping, pounding footsteps. Hundreds of them – still in the distance but coming closer, and coming quickly – a rumbling noise like a stampede of wild animals. Surrounding the sound, surging and ebbing in waves, was a noise like a low vicious howl.

Harrigan got to his feet slowly, moving like a man entranced. He turned so that he was facing back down the road, and he stood, rooted to the ground, and raised one big beefy hand to his brow to shield his eyes from the glare of sunlight.

I realized the enormous danger an instant too late – one single second of carelessness that I could never get back.

Two shots rang out, clear as bells in the still morning air, the sound of each one separated by no more than a breath. The first bullet zinged off the roof of the car in a jagged blade of sparks. The second shot struck Harrigan in the temple, an inch above his ear. The contents of his skull blew out through the side of his head in a pink cloud of blood. He dropped like a stone, dead on the grassy lawn even before I could reach him.

"No!" I shouted. Harrigan's body hit the ground and the ruined shattered remains of his head lolled to face me. There was blood everywhere and his features were no longer recognizable. His jaw hung loose, his skull collapsed. "God, no!"

I knelt in the long grass staring down at Harrigan's body. I reached for his hand. It was heavy and still warm. I wrapped my fingers around his, and I felt a sudden fierce inferno of fury burn through my soul. The anger came like a fire-storm – a blaze of hatred and vehemence unlike anything I had ever known.

Rage blinded me. I groped for a gun. The Glock was in the grass beside Harrigan's body. I snatched at it, and above the rising storm of my anger, I heard myself screaming.

I got to my feet, the gun clenched tightly in both fists, and fired at the house across the street, blazing gunfire and crying out in anger. The gun slammed back in my hand and the air seemed to shake with the snap of each shot. Tears welled in my eyes and stung like sweat. I fired again and again until suddenly my legs were taken from under me in a tackle that punched up beneath my ribs and slammed me hard on my back to the ground.

Jed's face was twisted in anger, pressed right above mine, the weight of him driving the wind from my lungs. "Enough!" he spat. "We've got to get inside the house!"

He shook me. He grabbed the front of my shirt and smacked the back of my head into the ground. "Understand?"

The fight went out of me, replaced by something cold and hollow – something that gnawed like acid in my guts. I blinked away tears.

Jed rolled off me and I sat up, despairing and desolate, and looked about me numbly.

"You'll have to carry Walker," I said, but the words were flat and listless. "It will take too long dragging him on the blanket."

Jed rubbed his chin and his eyes got hard.

"Leave him," he said. "That's what he wants anyhow. Leave him a gun and take the girl."

"No," I shook my head. "Harrigan is dead. Walker we are going to save."

Jed scrabbled close and his words were harsh and brutal in my ear. "He's as good as dead already, fucker! He just hasn't stopped breathing yet. Leave him here."

"I said no," I glared back at him.

Jed's expression transformed slowly, darkening with insolent defiance. His eyes narrowed to vicious little slits, but not enough to hide the malevolence that lurked there in the shadows of his mind.

I felt my fingers tightening around the Glock. I felt the cold ice in my veins begin to harden.

The moment hung on a knife-edge.

And then there was a roar in the distance – a wailing, keening sound, prehistoric and primeval that shredded the tension, and replaced it with something even more primitive – the inherent instinct for survival.

The undead had reached the gentle rise in the road. They came sweeping across the crest in a wall of dark seething death, lured towards us by the insatiable thirst for blood, driven to frenzy by the scent of Harrigan's murdered body and the furious roar of echoing gunfire.

I grabbed for the girl's wrist and pulled her close against me. Jed scrambled to his haunches. He took hold of Walker's arm, ready to heave him up and over his back.

"This will probably kill him," Jed grunted. "You know that, don't you?"

I didn't answer. Jed grunted and struggled until Walker hung like a sack of potatoes across his broad shoulders. He was straining to stay under the cover of the car. His jaw was clenched, the muscles in his chest and biceps bulging under the enormous strain. Then he started to run.

I waited until Jed was half-way across the lawn, holding the girl like she was on a tether, while she squirmed and pulled against me in a desperate panic to flee. As soon as Jed's feet hit the concrete path that led to the front door, I sprang to my feet and pushed the girl ahead of me, using my body to shield her, carrying the heavy nylon bag in one hand and my Glock in the other.

I heard a single shot, and I felt my body tense – felt every muscle clench, expecting to be thrown forward by the crushing impact as the bullet slogged into the broad of my back. But it never came. The shot went wide, and the gun fell silent.

I snatched a glance over my shoulder. The undead were splintering apart, as those that moved more fluidly began to break away from the hunting pack. They were pounding towards us, clawing at the air as if it might speed them on, straining with the mindlessness of a raw thirst for blood.

I turned and hurled myself through the front door of the house.

We were standing in a small square living room full of furniture that looked like it had been bought second-hand. There was an armchair and a small television set on a chipped and worn timber table. At either end of the table was a bunch of religious statues. The room was hot and airless. I could smell grime and dirt in the carpets. Jed looked at me and then started to ease Walker from his shoulders.

"No!" I said. "We're not staying."

"We're not?"

"No. Keep moving. Out the back door."

"Are you fucking crazy?"

I didn't have time for long explanations. "Once they tear Harrigan's body to shreds, they'll come looking for us. We need to put space between the body and us. Now move it!"

We went down a mean narrow hallway. There were plenty of doors on either side, but we didn't stop. All the doors were hanging open. At the back of the house was an eat-in kitchen that smelled of grease and grime and stale cooking odors. I flung the back door open and went down three wooden steps into the yard. The girl was close behind me. She held the door wide open and Jed came out like a wounded bull, still with Walker hanging from his shoulders, and his face wrenched into a grimace of agony.

The yard was a riot, overgrown with grass and creeping vines. It was what a garden becomes after years of neglect.

I went left towards a fence. It was sagging against its upright posts, the palings stained and brittle like a mouthful of old teeth. I kicked out with the flat of my foot and the timbers shattered with a sound like chicken bones.

"Get through," I snapped at the girl. She ducked through the gap obediently and turned, ashen faced and shaking. I pulled two more of the palings off with my hands and then went through the gap. I turned back and Jed lowered Walker from his shoulders and I helped him get the big man into the next yard. Walker's body was unnaturally hot, the heat burning through the fabric of his clothes, and his face was glistening with the perspiration of a man in the grips of fever. I thrust my fingers under his jaw and felt a fluttering pulse that was thin and reedy and uncertain.

Jed came and slid his big hands under Walker's armpits and I took up the weight of his legs. Walker groaned and stiffened in pain, but I ignored it. I clamped his ankles together and we carried him like that through long grass and over rock bed gardens to the back fence of the property.

There was a speedboat in the yard, tied down to a trailer and covered with a grimy canvas tarpaulin that had been daubed with bird droppings and fallen leaves. The fence itself was like something from a farm; a row of treated wooden posts, strung through with thick wire. Beyond the fence I could see the back of another house.

"There," I said in a ragged breath. "We need to get him into that house."

We heaved Walker's prone body over the fence, and I had to screw down tight on my rising panic, fearing the sight of marauding undead as the seconds dragged inexorably on.

When we reached the back door we set Walker carefully down.

The house was low and sprawling with dark cedar siding and insect screens on all the windows. All the windows were dark, curtains drawn. I could see a thick stone chimney rising through the roof. Insects buzzed around my ears and I felt flies crawl across my face. I swatted them away. The heat beat down on my shoulders like a steelyard furnace.

I glanced at Jed. He drew the Glock from inside the waistband of his jeans and pulled back on the slide.

"We go in hard and fast," he said, inflecting the words with a savage snarl. "No mercy. If there's anyone inside, we shoot to kill and ask questions later."

I nodded. I turned quickly to the girl. "Stay here with Walker."

Jed took two paces back then launched the heel of his boot at the door, aiming at a place an inch below the old lock. The door exploded inwards, smashed back hard against its hinges, the wood around the handle splintering.

His momentum carried him in through the door. He disappeared into dark gloom and I leaped into the gap right behind him, Glock drawn. I expected to be overwrought with tension and fear – but I wasn't. Somehow, something had altered. Somehow, Harrigan's death had changed me. I was detached, and remote, my gun hand steady, my breathing deep but regular.

We stepped through a laundry, into a kitchen and then down a short hallway to the living room. The house was silent. Not quiet – not like someone was sleeping.

It was deadly silent.

The house looked like it had been extended some time in the past because beyond the central core of rooms that seemed quite orderly, we suddenly stepped into a new hallway with a warren of small rooms branching out from it in unpredictable ways.

Jed and I checked every room and did it in two minutes flat. The house was empty of life, and empty of dead bodies.

The house was abandoned, but not in a ransacked, panicked way. It was as if the owners had left on holiday and simply never returned.

We went back out through the laundry and carried Walker inside. The change in temperature was immediate and dramatic. It was at least fifteen degrees cooler indoors. We carried him through to the biggest bedroom and laid him out on the mattress.

We had put distance and direction between Harrigan's body and us, but I sent Jed back through the house to barricade the front and back doors. He came back wincing, clutching at his ribs, a few minutes later.

"Done," he said. "They won't get through the back door. I've blocked it with the washing machine, and it weighs a ton. And I put a chest of drawers across the front door."

I nodded. "You okay?"

"I'll live."

Walker's eyes fluttered, his eyelids heavy like he was drifting off to sleep – or maybe worse. I slapped his face with my open hand and shook his shoulder.

"Leave him!" Jessica said suddenly. She flew at me, and clawed at my arms, but I pushed her aside and then turned on her venomously.

"Stand right there," I hissed. "Because you're next."

There must have been something in my voice, or maybe in the cold dangerous way I glared at her. She shrunk away from me, backed into a corner of the bedroom and all the defiance went out of her like a gasp of breath. I turned back to Walker and shook him again. His eyes came open, dull and unfocussed. They searched across the ceiling uncertainly, then settled on my face, leaning over the bed.

"What's your name?" I demanded. "Your real name?"

"Walker," he said.

"And you're Secret Service?"

He swallowed and then nodded.

"And who is the girl?"

"I told you," he said, his voice straining.

"Tell me again."

There was a long pause, but I didn't feel he was stalling. I felt like he was summoning the last reserves of his strength. "Jessica Steinman," Walker said. "She's the Vice President of America's daughter. I was assigned to get her out of Washington – to get her to safety."

"Where were you flying to?"

177

"Pentelle," Walker said. "Like I told you. There are navy ships off Norfolk. Her father is there, and a couple of the Joint Chiefs."

"Where is the President? Where is the rest of the government?"

"Dead," Walker said. "There is no government." He started to shiver. The head wound was seeping fresh blood, soaking through the thin bandage of his shirt. I didn't know what else was wrong with him. Maybe broken legs. Probably internal injuries. Jed shredded a pillow case into long strips and I bound the rags around Walker's forehead.

I snatched a bottle of water from the nylon bag and held it up to his lips. He drank thirstily.

"The helicopter was flying us to Pentelle," Walker went on. "It got into trouble."

"That's why it was painted black, right? Because you were carrying the Vice President's daughter."

Walker nodded – a barely perceptible movement of his head. "There was no pilot charging thousands of dollars for flights, was there?"

"No," Walker admitted. "We were one of the last flights out of the Capitol. It was done in secrecy. I was under direct orders from the Vice President to get his daughter to safety. It was covert."

"And the pilot?"

"Secret Service," Walker said.

"You shot him."

Walker's eyes suddenly went wide with surprise. He said nothing.

I leaned over him and stared into his eyes. "I checked the pilot's body when we reached the helicopter," I said, and my voice took on an edge of menace. "It was the first thing I did, Walker. He was dead in his harness. He had a bullet hole in his chest. I felt it."

Walker held my gaze for a few more seconds, and then nodded. "When the chopper crashed, the first thing I did was check Jessica, and then the pilot. He was already dead," Walker said. "So I shot him through the back of the seat."

"Why?" I was incredulous.

"Blood," Walker said. "There were zombies coming from the houses on the hill. We could see them backlit by the fires. I knew my only hope of getting Jessica to safety would be if I used the pilot's dead body to distract them. So I shot him. Then I saw you and the others come running from one of the houses. I hit myself on the head with the butt of the gun and threw it aside."

I looked up at Jed and saw my surprise and shock reflected in his expression. I stared back down at Walker.

"That's why you came alert so quickly when we reached you in the wreckage. You were faking."

He nodded.

"And that's why you were shouting," I suddenly realized. "When we pulled you from the helicopter you were shouting about your daughter."

Walker nodded again. "Jessica was unconscious. I knew when she came too, she would need to know the cover story."

"The story about her being your daughter."

Walker nodded.

I sat back again and stared up at the ceiling, then glanced malevolently over my shoulder at Jessica Steinman. "And you were in on this? You played along every inch of the way."

She said nothing. I took a deep breath.

Walker coughed weakly and bloody spittle trickled from the corner of his mouth. I suddenly didn't care.

"And the story about your wife?" I asked through a rising sense of outrage. "The story about your poor wife being trapped in your house by undead. Was that fake too? Were the tears faked, Walker?"

He nodded. "I made it up," he said. "All of it."

For some ridiculous, illogical reason, this betrayal enraged me more than any other deception. Perhaps it was because Jed and Harrigan and I had all lost precious loved ones. The pain was real and raw for us – and this Secret Service assassin had cheapened their deaths with his deceit.

Like I said, it made no logical sense – but the sudden hatred that overwhelmed me was so intense, I felt my hands bunch into angry fists.

I pressed my face close to his until just a few inches separated us. I glared at him hatefully. "I hope you die, you bastard," I whispered.

I got up from the bed and turned to Jessica Steinman. "Come with me," I snapped.

I took her out into the kitchen. I wanted her away from Walker. She followed me like a condemned man on his way to the gallows. I pressed her up against a wall and stood over her, my arms folded, simmering with a poisonous cocktail of emotions.

Jed drifted into the room casually but kept his distance. The girl stared up into my face, her enormous dark eyes like twin pools of fear and despair.

"What happened just before the helicopter crashed?" I demanded.

She frowned, like she didn't understand the question. "The helicopter was spinning out of control," she said softly. "There was smoke in the cabin. The pilot was screaming at me to hold on to something."

"And when it hit the ground – did the pilot die instantly?"

Jessica shook her head. "I don't know," she said. "I was knocked out. I don't remember anything until the moment I saw your face leaning over me."

I backed away a pace and lowered the intensity of my voice. "Are you really Vice President Steinman's daughter?"

She nodded. "Yes."

"And is he really on a warship off the coast?"

She nodded again. "He came back with the fleet from the Middle East," she said. "He had been on a diplomatic mission to Afghanistan and Iraq through most of June."

"And you stayed in Washington? Why didn't you go with him? I see the President's kids on the television all the time travelling on Air Force One. Why did you stay behind?"

She shrugged her shoulders. "I had studies, and I was helping my step-mother with a fundraiser for returned veterans…"

"Your mother?"

"Step mother," Jessica corrected me pointedly. "She's dead. She died when the Capitol was overrun."

"I'm sorry."

"Don't be."

There was a brief pause. "How did you survive?" I asked.

"I was in a bunker for almost three weeks," Jessica went on. "When the navy ships with my father aboard reached the coast, they started ferrying people to Pentelle – or directly offshore to the fleet. I wouldn't leave until the others had been evacuated first. Walker stayed with me and the helicopter we were on was the last one."

"And I suppose you think that makes you some kind of a hero?" I asked. It was churlish, I suppose, but I wanted to vent at this girl for being part of Walker's deception – for putting all our lives in danger without ever telling us the truth.

But I couldn't.

She had done what her bodyguard had told her, even though she had been clearly terrified out of her mind. She had maintained her silence – and her discipline – through two days of terrible fear. Grudgingly, I had to respect her – but I didn't want to. I wanted to hate her.

Jessica didn't answer. Her eyes flicked to where Jed was standing, and then back to me. Maybe she was wondering about her safety now that Walker was so badly injured. Maybe she was wondering what we were going to do with her.

She took a deep tremulous breath, like she was getting herself under control, and then she looked up at me with a clear steady gaze.

"Before we left Washington, Mr Walker gave me this," she said and held out her arm. The big chunky bracelet dangled from her narrow wrist. "It's a homing beacon of some sort," she said, "made to look like a piece of jewelry."

I had noticed this bracelet before. Now I took her hand and twisted it, studying the floral pattern more closely. It looked like it was made of something like pewter. The latch at the back of the chain was peculiar.

"How does it work?" Jed asked the question.

Jessica shrugged. "I don't know," she admitted. "All I know is that it's some kind of beacon. If I activate it, it sends out a message or radio signal on a military frequency to anyone nearby."

"How nearby?" I asked.

"Mr Walker said it was about ten miles," Jessica said.

"And it's a military frequency?"

She nodded. "That's what he said. He said if we got within ten miles of Pentelle, the navy helicopters would be able to find us."

"Then why not activate it right now? Why not get the navy here to pick us all up?"

"Have you heard any helicopters?" she shook her head. "There are none. The navy is only flying survivors who make it to Pentelle, out to the waiting warships. There aren't any helicopters left for search missions. That's what Mr Walker

183

said before we left the Capitol. It's why it was so important that we made it to Pentelle."

"No helicopters to spare? Not even for the daughter of the Vice President?"

She shrugged and stared at me. "How would that look?" she asked cynically. "How would the other survivors react if they knew my father was sending helicopters across the countryside looking for his missing daughter while their friends and loved ones might be trapped somewhere in just as much need and just as much danger?"

She had a point.

Jed stepped closer. I could smell the sweaty odor of his body. "Does the bracelet come off your wrist?" he asked. Perhaps it was my imagination, but I sensed something sinister in his tone, as if cunning thoughts were forming in his mind.

Jessica shook her head. Her hair swished across her shoulders. "No," she said. "There's some kind of lock…"

"Like one of those house arrest ankle bracelets?"

Jessica shrugged. I wasn't sure she even knew what Jed was talking about.

Jed frowned thoughtfully, then stepped back, turned and looked out through the curtains – the action had become almost as instinctive as breathing. Then he went to the refrigerator and pulled open the door.

The stench of rotting food was awful. Jed recoiled and wrinkled his nose. He slammed the door shut.

I turned back to Jessica, my temper cooled. "Go back and check on Walker," I said. "Make him comfortable and see if he wants more water. We'll join you in a couple of minutes."

She scurried from the room, almost grateful to be gone. I waited until I knew she was well out of earshot, and I turned to Jed.

He spoke first. "That kid is our meal-ticket to safety," he said. "She's going to buy us our freedom."

I raised my eyebrows. "Really?"

He nodded and looked smug. "When we get her to safety, we'll be heroes," Jed said.

"Really?" I asked again. I wasn't so sure. "And what if she sets off her little transmitter and a big fat navy chopper lands to pick her up – but they won't take us? What happens then, little brother?"

Jed smiled bleakly. "We hold her hostage."

"As simple as that?"

Jed nodded.

"I thought you might just cut her arm off, Jed. Then we could travel more easily and activate the transmitter when we get near Pentelle," I said, my words dripping with sarcasm.

"Thought about it," Jed said matter-of-factly. "But I don't think the chopper would land. And I don't think they would pick us up. They'll be expecting the kid."

I stared at him, and I had no doubt that he had seriously considered amputating the girl's arm as an option.

When we went back into the bedroom, somehow Walker looked worse. His face was the color of marble, glistening with beads of perspiration. He was lying under a sheet, shivering through clenched teeth, as though he were in the grips of some terrible fever. I touched his cheek and it was hot.

There was a bottle of water on the bed beside him. Jessica sat on the edge of the mattress, her face furrowed with desperate worry and helplessness. She looked up at me. Her eyes were huge and haunted.

"We're getting out of here," I said. I wasn't sure Walker was lucid enough to hear me, but I made my voice sound confident and determined for the girl's sake. "We're getting you to Pentelle."

Jessica looked doubtful. "Mr Walker?"

"He's coming with us," I said firmly. But I didn't add, *'if he lives long enough.'*

"When?" she fidgeted with the bracelet anxiously, like she was desperate to activate the beacon.

"Early tomorrow morning," I declared. "A couple of hours before sunrise, I'm going out to get a vehicle."

And revenge.

Chapter Five.

"This ain't a smart thing you're doing," my brother said. He was leaning in the doorway of the living room. He had a bottle of rum in his hand.

He had spent the afternoon ransacking the house. He had found a hunting knife, and a liquor cabinet.

He had spent the evening drinking.

For the first couple of hours he was voluble, and expansive, but as the night dragged on, his mood had become somber. Now he stood in the doorway, swaying ever so slightly, and staring at me with red-raw eyes and an expression that was like thunder.

"We don't have a choice," I said. I had found dark pants, and a black t-shirt. I pulled them on and shrugged my leather jacket back over my shoulders. "We can't stay here. We need to get to Pentelle. To do that, we need a car."

Jed nodded. We had been over this ground before. "But going out on your own…? Man, that's stupid."

"Do you think I want to?" I snapped hotly. "Jed, there isn't another option. You can't go on your own – your ribs are all banged up, and you can't come with me because that would leave the Vice President's daughter and her dying body guard alone in the house," I said dramatically. "There's no other choice. I have to go out and find a car."

I snatched up the Glock, made sure the magazine was full, and pulled back the slide to chamber a round. The mechanism made an ominous *'click-clack'* noise that sounded obscenely loud in the heavy silence.

I strode purposefully past Jed and headed for the bedroom. He followed me.

Jessica was perched on the edge of the bed, staring blankly into empty space. She was holding Walker's hand. The man lay prone and perfectly still under the sheet. He wasn't shivering any more, and he wasn't sweating. I didn't think that was a good sign, but I said nothing. A candle was burning on a low dresser, spilling soft yellow light around the room.

Jessica turned her head slowly towards me. Her eyes were red and puffy and her cheeks slick with tears. She had been weeping.

"I'm going to get a car," I said. "Something reliable and in good condition that will get us all to Pentelle."

Jessica looked suddenly alarmed. Her eyes flicked instinctively to where Jed stood in the background, then quickly back to me. She shook her head, like she was in a dazed state of denial. "No!" she said vehemently. "You can't leave us."

"I'm not," I said. I didn't have time for this. The sun would rise in a couple of hours. I wanted to be away. The fear of going out into the zombie-filled night had been churning in my guts throughout the afternoon. Now I just wanted to get it done. "I'm going to get a car. I'm coming back for you – and for Walker."

She sprang from the bed and took a step towards me. There was desperation and panic in her eyes, but then she stopped in mid-stride and the energy seemed to leave her like she had been punctured. She sagged and grabbed for the bed. Big fat tears were rolling down her cheeks.

I crouched down in front of her, lifted her chin in my hand until she was looking at me through glistening damp eyes. "I will be back," I said firmly. "Before you know it."

I got up and went out through the bedroom door, the sound of Jessica sobbing following my steps like a haunting ghost. At the front door of the house I stopped and turned round to face Jed.

"Two hours," I said grimly, "maybe sooner. While I'm gone I need you to get Walker into this room. Lay him out on the floor and get him ready. Get the girl to help you. It will give her something to do – keep her occupied."

Jed nodded but said nothing.

"When I pull up out front, you're going to need to be quick," I went on. "There could be undead all around us. You'll need to get Walker and the girl out to the car, so be ready to go at a moment's notice. Understand?"

Jed nodded again. He took a long swig from the bottle of rum. He wiped his mouth with the back of his hand. "What happens if you don't come back? What if you don't make it?"

"I'll be back," I said confidently. "But if something goes wrong, and I don't get back here within two hours, you need to get Walker and Jessica to Pentelle – any way you can."

I had lit a candle at sunset and perched it on a bookshelf that had been set against one wall. Now I blew it out, and the living room was plunged into darkness.

We shifted the chest of drawers barricade, and I cracked the front door open.

The sounds of night came to me, faint on the breeze: the rustle of insects and the soft, distant call of an owl. I narrowed my eyes and concentrated on the dark shapes scattered across the front lawn, wary of everything that might hide one of the undead.

I stood, waiting and watching, for a full minute with my heart pounding and my nerves strung tight to snapping point. My hands were damp with sweat, and the Glock felt like it was made of lead. I glanced over my shoulder at the dark specter that was my brother's face.

"Remember. Two hours," I whispered. "If I'm not back by then, I'm dead. Get the girl and Walker to Pentelle. Be a hero, Jed."

I crept out into the night.

* * *

I went across the lawn in a low running crouch and stopped when the gnarled shape of a low shrub suddenly loomed out the darkness. I hunched down beside it, using the bush for cover, and listened carefully for sounds above the racing beat of my heart. The night was clear, and there was a big chunk of moon quite low in the sky. The stars seemed impossibly bright and their ambient light gave me some kind of visibility up to about fifteen feet at which I could define differences in the shadows.

I waited just long enough for my breathing to settle, and then I doubled back on my tracks, turning to move down the side of the house towards the back yard.

The house had been built just a few feet from the neighboring fence. There was no path. Instead I waded through long tangling vines and heavy clumps of grass. Every step was a new sound. Every pace I took was fraught with tension. But I kept one hand on the fence to guide me and reached the rear corner of the house without incident.

Another moment of hesitation – this time to get my bearings. Jed and I had carried Walker across this lawn earlier in the day, but under the heavy cloak of night everything looked very different. I knew in my mind where the fences were and I struck out across the grass, trying to move in a straight line – trying to re-trace our steps from earlier in the day.

I was heading back towards where Clinton Harrigan had died.

It had been several hours, but the grief and sadness of the big gentle Christian man's loss was still upon me, like a black shroud. I knew that returning to the scene of his murder was filled with danger, but I didn't think that danger would be lingering hordes of undead. I doubted they would be still massed on the street, nor that they would be still gathered around the shredded remains of his body. I was gambling they had drifted away in search of new prey.

Gambling with my life.

I figured it took me fifteen or maybe twenty minutes of careful stealth to reach the house we had escaped into earlier that day – the house we had fled out through the back door without stopping. I reached the back step and looked up. The door was swinging open. I went up the steps carefully and pressed my ear against the wall.

I heard the creak of floorboards from somewhere inside the house – a noise like a mournful groan. My senses screamed in alarm. The sound was carrying towards me ahead of someone – or something's – footsteps. The footsteps stopped briefly and then came again.

I went back down the stairs quickly and scrambled to the corner of the house. My plan had been to go back through the house, and then out onto the lawn to reach the wrecked car where Harrigan had been shot. But the sound of footsteps frightened the hell out of me, and I knew that if I got cornered and was confronted, any chance of carrying out my plan would be destroyed in a blaze of panicked gunfire.

I crept along the side of the house, with one hand against the cold abrasive texture of the bricks and the other extended way out in front of me, clinging tightly to the Glock.

At the front corner of the house was a narrow gate made of white wooden pickets and topped with a screen of lattice timber. It was too high to climb, and I couldn't go around, unless I climbed the neighbor's fence. I groped around in the eerie silent gloom until I felt the latch and unfastened it.

I inched the gate open with my jaw clenched and my face screwed up into a fearful wince. The hinges groaned a little as the gate swung – and then screeched loudly in sudden ear-piercing resistance. The sound rang out into the night like a blood-curdling scream.

My heart stopped beating.

When it started again, it was pounding faster than any human body could possibly endure. I was in an ice-cold lather of panic. The sound seemed to echo in the night and fade away slowly, and – fool that I am – I stood there like a deer caught in the headlights of a speeding car, waiting for precious seconds until the clamor of warning sirens going off in mind finally reached my legs.

I began to run.

I ran as fast as I could – straight across the front lawn towards the roadside where the shadow of the wrecked, mangled car loomed out of the starlit night like some prehistoric monster. I ran to get away from the piercing sound of the gate – but made noise I couldn't avoid in my fleeing panic. My breath sawed in my throat, my footsteps sounded loud as drums, and my arms pumped furiously. I saw a shifting, ethereal shape close to my left. It was a bush. I kept running. Another shifting shape, this one somehow denser, seemed to peel away from the hulking silhouette of the car wreckage. It lunged at me.

Too late I realized it was the figure of a woman, her hair a tangled mess, her hands seized into claws. I threw up my arm in a purely defensive gesture and felt the woman clasp hold of me with a grip like a vice. I lost all momentum. I felt myself being pulled off my feet. I heard the woman snarl and saw a flash of yellow teeth. She bit into the sleeve of my leather coat and her jaws locked tight. I screamed. We went over together on the soft spongy grass in a tangle of flailing, clawing arms and kicking legs. I went ice cold with fear. The woman snarled and thrashed her head from side to side, trying to burrow her teeth through the heavy leather. I flung up the Glock and jammed the barrel against her face. I pulled the trigger and fell scrambling backwards as the woman's head exploded in a great gout of dark gore.

I crawled to the curb. My hands were shaking uncontrollably. My legs wouldn't work. Fear had turned my limbs to jelly.

I got as far as the wrecked car. The night was filling with strange noises – the rising sound of warning voices like jungle drums becoming louder and sounding closer.

I scrambled on my hands and knees in the gutter, working my way in a panic to the front of the flat-bed truck we had rear-ended. The side of the road was a littered mess of broken headlight glass, shards of twisted metal and gravel that crunched under my boots. I reached the front fender of the truck and crouched there.

Dark shapes were gathering further down the road – shapes still too distant to have substance or definition. They coalesced and seemed to writhe like black smoke, forming and then breaking apart.

I charged across the street like a sprinter out of the blocks, running as fast as my shaking legs would carry me, directly towards a two-story brick house.

I reached the dark cover of dense shrubs and I burrowed low seeking the safety of the shadows. But I didn't relax.

This was the house the gunman who killed Clinton Harrigan had fired from.

My nerves stayed tightly strung, my senses heightened, cranked all the way into the red zone by my fear... and an underlying cold implacable urge for retribution. I felt the anger within me grinding like gears.

There was a narrow belt of long grass stretched out before me, then an equally narrow area with more low shrubs and bark chips. Then, down a narrow walkway, there was the front porch of the house. I went left instead. A driveway wound down the side of the home and wrapped behind the back of the building. At the end of the drive was a two-car garage. The roller doors were down. I didn't try to lift either of them. There was a small window cut into the side wall of the garage. I pressed my nose against the glass and cupped my hands close around my face. There was a hulking dark shadow inside the structure.

I turned away and studied the back of the house. The moon hung over the distant treetops, casting everything in a ghostly grey glow. It was enough for me to make out the shape of a long porch and a wide set of three steps leading up to the back door.

I went to the steps. They were a basic wooden assembly. I went up one step at a time, treading carefully, keeping my weight on the edges of each board where they had been nailed to the side rail to minimize the risk of them creaking.

The porch was wide and littered with worn sofa chairs, wooden crates and old bicycle parts. The back door had a weary old screen door fixed in front of it with tears in the sagging gauze. A rusted spring mechanism held the door closed. I pulled it back slowly, expecting the worst, but the spring had lost all its tension. It gave way without a sound and I pulled the screen door all the way open.

I pressed my ear against the back door and listened. It was just a plain hollow slab with a rectangle of painted beading. The paint was peeling. I stood silently for a few seconds but heard nothing.

My instincts told me to wait. I remembered something about caution being the better part of valor, but the fact was that I expected the entire street to be over-run with convulsing undead at any moment.

I couldn't wait.

It was do or die….

I held the Glock ready, then took two steps back and launched my foot at the door in a side kick that had all my strength behind it. The door blew inwards and the noise was like a sudden loud explosion.

I went through the opening without hesitating.

And tripped over a dead body.

Even in the darkness I knew it was a body, and I knew it was dead. My foot socked into it and I fell face-first on top of cold stinking flesh. The gun flew from my hand. I heard it skitter away across the floor.

The body must have been stretched out on its back. My fingers dug into rubbery resistance, and then my hand groped over facial features and long greasy hair. I felt a sudden surge of nausea rise up into the back of my throat. My fingers came away covered in oozing slime and I felt my skin crawl. I scrambled away from the corpse and then went stone cold when I felt the barrel of a gun suddenly thrust hard down against the top of my head.

"Stay on your knees," a man's voice said tensely from out of the darkness. I froze. I heard heavy rasping breathing, and then the voice ghosted out of the night again, this time dripping with undisguised relish. "You're fucked."

I turned my head a little and caught the shape of the man in the corner of my eye. He was holding a flashlight, the glow from the bulb muted by wads of tissue paper so that the light it gave off was like a child's bedroom nightlight. I couldn't see him clearly until he stepped past me and pushed the back door closed. I heard the scrape of an iron bar, and then the sound of it being set between steel brackets. The man turned quickly back to face me and suddenly I could see past the glow of the flashlight.

He was ghastly.

He was a small, wiry man, maybe seventy – maybe even older. He was shirtless, and the skin of his chest was wrinkled and sagging, the flesh on his arms hung in loose folds. The man's face was drawn, the skin pallid. He leered at me and I realized he had no teeth. There was spittle dribbling down his chin.

He was wearing the decapitated head of a dead man, tied by rope and knotted under his chin. The dead man's head had long wiry black hair, the eye sockets empty, the mouth open and its purple swollen tongue protruding obscenely.

The gunman was wearing the dead man's head like some kind of grotesque Easter bonnet.

"Get up," the old man said. He was wheezing – the sound of his breath being choked by bad lungs. I got to my feet.

"Start walkin'," the old man said. He jabbed the barrel of the gun between my shoulder blades. "There's a candle in the living room. Walk towards the light... and do it slow like."

I went in a careful shuffle. The house was dark, but I could see the faintest glow bouncing off internal walls. We went through a dilapidated kitchen with carefully packed cardboard boxes lined up along the worn linoleum floor. The house stank of decay and urine. I reached a doorway and turned left then right until I stepped into a large room with timber floorboards. The room was completely empty. No furniture, no paintings or photos on the wall.

No windows.

The candle was set on a three-foot high steel stand in the middle of the floor. I went towards it and when I was standing beside the flickering glow, the man called from somewhere behind me.

"Stop right there. Turn around."

I turned.

He was hovering in the shadows on the edge of the room, his shape blurred by the darkness. He switched the flashlight off and there was a long silence.

"Take off the jacket, and the t-shirt," the old man's words ghosted out of the gloom. I hesitated, and he barked the order again, his voice snapping.

I peeled off the leather jacket and let it fall to the floor. Then I pulled off the t-shirt and tossed it aside. I stood there, bare-chested, and he stepped out from the darkness towards me, with the gun in his hand pointed between my eyes.

He was a skeletal figure, his face lined and deeply creased like old wood. The hair of his beard had fallen out in tufts leaving clods of white strands that were stained dirty brown around the corners of his mouth and down his chin. He looked me up and down carefully, and the decapitated head, strapped to his chin like a hideous helmet, bobbed and swayed precariously.

The man was wearing nothing but a pair of dirty underpants. He had scrawny white hairless legs, and a bizarre mat of grey hair that trailed down the hollow curve of his chest to the base of his stomach.

"Who are you?" he pointed a finger at me.

"I'm one of the people you shot at on the road outside," I said.

He looked suddenly astonished. His eyes widened.

"You murdered my friend," I said.

The old man's head nodded like it was being jerked at the end of a puppeteer's string – as if he was recalling a fond memory. "The fat one."

"His name was Clinton. Clinton Harrigan." I had to grit my teeth and fight back the impulse to charge across the space that separated us. "He was a good man. A kind man – and you shot him dead."

The old man's eyes rolled from side to side, and he cackled with delight so that I could see the broken rotting black stumps of his teeth. He danced away from me in some kind of mad jig, then spun back and thrust one of his hands down inside the sagging elastic band of his underpants. His eyes went wide and rolled up into the top of his skull.

He was insane.

The old man sighed, and then licked his lips. "How much do you weigh?" he asked, and his voice was breathless and slurred. "One eighty? One ninety?"

I said nothing, but I felt a sudden cold chill of impending doom. The man waved the gun in my face and then the madness in his eyes seemed to recede. They turned hard as stone. He glowered at me.

"Pick up the candle," he snapped. "Go down the hall. At the end, turn left."

I took the candle off its stand and for the flash of a split-second I considered turning on the old man and smashing my fist in his face. But he was insane – not stupid. He kept himself out of reach, and I knew I wouldn't be fast enough to whirl round on him before he could kill me.

I went down the hall. The candle flame flickered and huge distorted shadows played and leaped across the dark walls. At the end of the hall was another passageway. I turned left, and the floor beneath my feet felt suddenly sticky.

The crazy old man jabbed me in the back with the gun. "At the end of the hall is a door. Open it and go down the stairs."

The door was like something from a medieval dungeon. It was made of solid timber with huge iron-strap hinges. There was a heavy black metal ring for a handle. I pulled the door open and a nauseous brew of ripe rotting smells washed over me from a basement.

A descending set of stone stairs stretched out before me. They were well lit with candle light. The steps were rough stone, like they had been fashioned without care, hewn from solid rock.

"Move," the old man hissed.

I went down the steps slowly, my fear rising as I descended. I heard the old man pull the door firmly shut behind us.

It was an underground cavern, torn from the rock beneath the house. The walls were ragged, the floor covered in hard crusted dirt. The whole area was lit up by hundreds of candles, like a macabre altar. The flickering light leaped up the walls and cast everything in it with a golden glow and deep menacing shadows.

There was an old table set in one corner, and on it I saw some kind of a jacket. There were sewing needles and reels of cotton. There were plastic buckets under the table.

Beside the table was a long cement trough, streaked and stained with blood, and above it – suspended from their ankles on huge iron hooks – hung three dead bodies.

"What the fuck…?" I gasped. The words were wrenched impulsively, and were numbed with my incredulous horror. I felt my eyes widen with shock.

There were two women's bodies, and between them hung the corpse of a man. Each body had its wrists slashed. The women had their throats cut. The man's head had been hacked from its neck.

They were all naked, dripping the last drops of their blood into the trough. The corpses had been cut behind the Achilles tendon, and meat hooks buried into each ankle to take the weight. Their legs were spread apart, with their feet wider apart than their shoulders. The women's throats had been cut from ear to ear, slicing through the neck and larynx, and severing the internal and external carotid arteries that carried blood from the heart to the head and brain.

One of the women had been skinned. Her stomach was deeply gouged where a knife had been inserted above the breast bone and then sliced down through the connecting tissue and muscle to peel long ragged flaps of flesh away from the corpse.

On a blood-stained bench beside the hanging bodies were several knives and a canvas sheet where the flesh had been stretched out and laid flat.

"Meet the family," the old man said. He nudged the closest corpse and it swayed like a slaughter yard carcass. "This is Ellie, my daughter, and at the other end, that's my wife, Marjory." He waved the gun around airily like a baton. "And that no-account son-bitch in the middle, that's Jethro, the daughter's boyfriend."

I backed away, stumbled in shock and disbelief. I felt the gorge of nausea rising in the back of my throat, scalding like acid. I clutched at the sewing bench and bent at the waist, heaving and retching painfully over my shoes and the dirt floor.

The old man sniggered.

I wiped my mouth with the back of my hand and stared numbly. My eyes were swimming and unfocussed. I shook my head to clear my senses and then realized the jacket on the bench was made of cured human flesh. The front and back of the hideous garment had been completed, and one sleeve attached with crude ragged stitches.

"They're your family?"

The old man shrugged.

I felt another dizzying bout of nausea rise up into my throat but I jammed down on the reflex and took short quick breaths, my mouth wide open, like a man who had run a marathon.

"You're insane," I choked, turning in outrage. "You're completely fucking insane!"

The old man turned his head quizzically and then frowned, almost like he didn't understand. The dead man's head he was wearing slipped down over his forehead and he pushed it back up with the tip of a gnarled, stained finger.

"I'm not insane," he said, offended. "I'm crazy. Crazy like a fox."

The gun in his hand became steady. He kept it pointed in the center of my chest. "The undead won't be able to sense me," he said softly. "Not if I'm wearing dead flesh. Once the clothes are complete, I'll be able to walk amongst them without being seen." He tapped his nose as if he were sharing some secret with me.

"You're mad..." I said again, this time more surely but he seemed not to notice. There was an evangelical blaze in his eyes like he was possessed.

"I wanted the fat one," the old man looked suddenly pained with disappointment. "He would have been enough to make the pants with flesh left over," he said, lamenting the fact that he had murdered Clinton Harrigan but not been able to retrieve the body. "That was a waste – like the other one in the back room who tried to break in last week. Had to shoot him of course, but I couldn't get the body down here. He was too heavy."

I leaned against the sewing bench. My head was spinning in a whirlpool of disbelief and horror.

"The man you murdered was my friend," I said.

The old man shrugged. "I needed the skin," he countered, and his tone was cold with the reasoning of insanity.

Slowly I felt the horror gradually uncoiling in my gut, becoming something darker. It rose, gathering size and strength and taking form until I could feel myself shaking with murderous rage. I felt my hands bunch into fists and a red mist of fury seemed to glaze over my eyes.

The old man was ten feet away. He was standing near the hanging corpse of one of the women. He crouched down to his haunches and dipped his hand into the blood-filled trough.

"The undead are driven to frenzy by the scent of blood," he said to me. He sucked the blood from one of his fingers and savored the taste like it was a rare delicacy. "It drives them mad. Did you know that?" Without waiting for an answer, he got back to his feet and gently fondled the breast of the dead woman. The corpse swayed gently, and the heavy hooks in her ankles groaned from their support beam in a low mournful creak. The man's breath hitched in his throat and his eyes rolled white into the back of his head. Without waiting for me to answer, he went on, his voice suddenly ragged with bizarre arousal. "That's why I use the basement," he said. "The walls are solid stone. They can't smell the blood down here."

He thrust his hand down inside his underpants and they fell down around his ankles while I stared in revulsion and disbelief. His brow furrowed in concentration and he blinked sweat from his eyes. He stared through me with a glazed wonder, his mouth open and dribbling, seeing something else entirely.

He groaned aloud. His dried out wrinkled body undulated lewdly, and he ran his hand through the coarse grey pelt of hair down to his sunken stomach in a grisly caress. He wrapped his fingers around the stub of his dangling penis and stroked himself. His skinny frame began to tremble uncontrollably and the shriveled pale flesh of him went hard within the dense unruly nest of pubic hair.

He groaned again, and a strangled sigh of ecstasy gurgled in his throat. Then he was gasping for breath, his chest heaving as he sagged on trembling legs.

I lunged for him.

I threw myself across the room, and there was a vicious, murderous roar in my ears – a sound I didn't recognize – a sound I didn't know I was capable of. I was shaking with rage, snarling like a wild animal, and my hands clawed around his skinny neck and buried viciously into the withered flesh of his throat.

The old man went backwards, crashing to the hard ground with my weight on top of him, driving the wind from his lungs. The gun fell from his hands and he kicked and thrashed in sudden fear and desperation. I drove my knee into his guts and hunched over him, feeling the tips of my fingers and my thumbs moving closer and closer together around his throat until they were almost touching – until the life would be choked out of him.

The old man's eyes were wide and wild. He made a sharp hissing sound. Spittle bubbled from his mouth and his eyes began to cloud over. I lifted his head and then smashed it back down into the ground. The decapitated head he was wearing fell off and rolled away, and I saw that the old man's thinning grey hair was matted stiff with dry blood.

He clawed at my hands and punched at my shoulder. He raked his nails down my forearm and scratched at my chest. I snarled at him – wild beyond reason – and beyond the reach of compassion or remorse. I shrugged his hands away and tightened my strangling grip around his throat.

I pounded the back of his skull hard down onto the ground again and he suddenly went slack. The breath escaped from him in a long weary wheeze, and his eyes seemed to bulge then glaze with mist. I opened my hands and drew away from him, shaking and gasping. The old man's gun was lying near the trough of blood. I scrambled for it on my hands and knees and snatched it up. I got to my feet and backed away, putting space between us. My hands were trembling, my body pumped full of adrenalin – but the brutal need for retribution still pounded like a relentless drumbeat in my head that I could not ignore.

I had never known an emotion so powerful as the need for revenge that gripped me.

"Get up," I said to the man.

He didn't move. He lay, limp and lifeless – but he was still breathing. I saw the gentle rise and fall of his chest.

"Get up," I repeated. "Get on your knees. Right now." I kicked out at him with my boot, and caught him high up on the thigh. His body flinched, and then he made a gargled choking sound in the back of his throat as though his lungs had suddenly started pumping again.

The old man groaned and reached for his throat. His breathing was harsh and asthmatic. He rolled his head and his eyes opened reluctantly. He saw me and there was a dark shadow of alarm in his gaze. He sat upright and then spasmed into a fit of coughing.

I held the gun on him and it was level and steady in my hand, as though carved from stone.

"I thought the zombie apocalypse was the horror to beat all horrors," I said conversationally, my voice flat and devoid of all emotion. "I thought nothing could be more terrifying than the undead rising to kill without remorse or reason. But I was wrong."

The man watched me uncertainly, his eyes flicking to the pistol in my hand.

"You changed all that." I paused. "You made me realize that despite the horror of an undead apocalypse, man is still the greatest threat, the worst danger – the most hideous, monstrous killer. And I can't let that continue. Not without fighting back for my friend who you murdered, and for the others whose lives you have taken because of your insanity."

"I did what I did to survive," the man said. "I did what any other would do."

I shook my head. "No, you went beyond that. You're a monster."

"You can't kill me. It would be murder!" the old man voice rose, becoming strident. "You would be just like me, and no better."

I smiled darkly. "I still retain my humanity," I said. "I don't know if you're insane. Maybe you are – but insanity doesn't excuse this… this atrocity, nor does it excuse the cold blooded murder of my friend. We might have been a civilized society before the apocalypse, but there was a time when an eye for an eye was the law. I'm bringing that back, as of right now." I heard the words in my own ears and they were formal and dispassionate, as though I were handing down an executioner's sentence.

I shifted my aim, lifting my arm a fraction until the barrel of the old man's gun was pointed between his eyes. He cringed away suddenly and threw his hands up in front of his face as if to shield himself from the bullet. He started to moan, and then the sound became the soft whimper of terrified sobbing.

"This isn't just revenge anymore," I said. "It was. Revenge is what brought me here. Revenge is what made me hunt you down. But now, it has become much more than that. This is a mercy killing. It's an execution because if I let you live, I know others will die at the hands of your madness."

I took three quick strides across the room towards him. The old man shrieked with fear and cowered away, backing up against the trough of blood so that the contents sloshed over the rim and spilled across the hard earth. When he could go no further, he snarled up into my eyes like a cornered beast, and shrieked a tirade of vicious abuse.

I put the gun to the top of his head.

I pulled the trigger.

The old man's skull exploded, spattering my legs with the contents. His withered body collapsed and went instantly limp beneath me while the roar of the gunshot in the confined space of the basement echoed off the walls and then finally faded.

The heavy silence afterwards was even more harrowing. I felt cold and empty and it tormented me. There was no swelling surge of triumph. There was no sense of vindication or justice. There was just the silence and my sickening despair. I cupped my face in my hands and my features felt worn and haggard, as if ravaged by some horrible disease.

I reeled away. My heart was thumping hard in my chest and my hands were shaking uncontrollably. There was a roar in my ears like the sound of crashing surf and I sweated and trembled with shock. I sucked in great lungsful of air, while the blood fizzed in my veins and the enormity of what I had done began to seep through the fading embers of my fury.

I turned away, shaken and shocked, and ran up the stairs. A clock in my head started ticking, counting down the seconds as I reached the big heavy door and slammed it shut behind me. There was a heavy steel bolt high up on the door that I had not noticed before. I hammered it into its iron bracket with the palm of my hand, sealing the hideous tomb, and then fled towards the kitchen.

I went straight for the cardboard boxes stacked carefully on the linoleum floor. They were packed with canned food, blankets, bottles of water and a flashlight. I tore the boxes to pieces in my haste and found a chunky set of keys.

I left everything behind, strewn across the floor, except the flashlight. I went to the back door and flung it open. The sky was filling with a dark brew of storm clouds that scudded in ragged tatters across the moon. The night was damp, but it wasn't raining. It was like the air was filled with a suspended drizzle, as if the rain hadn't quite arrived yet. I ran my fingers through the keys until I found two that were most likely to fit the garage roller doors. Then I burst from the house, and ran – literally – for my life.

I jammed the first key into the lock of the roller door. It went all the way in, but wouldn't turn. I reefed it out and thrust the second key in. The lock turned silently and I reached down and heaved the roller door all the way up.

Soft broken light filtered into the garage.

It was a large dark space with open rafters. It smelled of gasoline and fertilizer. One side seemed to be loaded up with tools and motor parts. I snapped the flashlight on for two seconds and bounced the light off the walls.

In the middle of the concrete floor was a Yukon. Maybe twelve years old. Maybe more. I could see the big GMC lettering across the grille. It was grey with dark tinted windows all round. The driver's side door was unlocked. I slid in behind the wheel. The seat was saggy, worn and tired with age and use, and the interior smelled of stale cigarette smoke. I found the car key and slid it into the ignition. Turned the key and the dials across the dashboard lit up.

I sat there and did nothing for three seconds – three precious seconds, torn and undecided.

"Fuck it!" I swore at last. I left the keys in the Yukon and the driver's door open. I ran to the side wall of the garage and groped around until I found a small can of lawn mower fuel. I shook it and heard the contents slosh. I guessed it was maybe half full.

More than enough.

I made a grim dash for the back of the house, suddenly overcome with the suicidal realization that I was risking more than just my own life – but it was too late. I went up the stairs and stepped over the dead body inside the door.

I splashed mower fuel through the kitchen and then spilled a trail to the back door. I still had Jed's cigarette lighter stuffed into the pocket of my pants. I put the lighter to the fuel and it went up with a soft *'whoosh'* in a fireball of flame and searing heat.

I ran.

I didn't look back.

I raced into the garage and hurled myself behind the wheel of the Yukon. The big engine thundered to life and I stomped my foot down on the gas. The tires screamed on the smooth surface of the concrete floor until the tread bit down in a burning feather of blue smoke. The Yukon leaped forward and I turned the wheel hard, roaring along the driveway with the door still swinging open.

Dark shapes were swarming from the street towards the house. They came from out of the night, convulsing and writhing, their twisted bodies driven by mindless rage and thirst. I saw them fill the windshield as the car crested the rise of the driveway and the road suddenly appeared beneath the big front wheels. I slewed the Yukon to the right, hauling the steering wheel hard over and grunting with alarm and fright. The front wheels washed into the loose stones in the gutter. The door was flung wide open and caught one of the undead ghouls with the impact of a swinging punch. It sent the zombie flailing backwards into the path of the surging horde behind it.

The Yukon swayed wildly on its suspension then righted itself, and the engine bellowed like wounded bull. The door slammed shut. The steering wheel was ripped from my hand and the car veered towards a mailbox on the opposite side of the street. I clawed it back, jounced up the curb and then felt my teeth slammed together as the car crashed and bounced back onto the road. The Yukon ploughed over the body of another undead ghoul that flashed across the windshield and then disappeared beneath the grille.

The clock in my head wasn't ticking any more.

It was broken.

How long had I been gone from the others? An hour? Maybe a little less…

Surely no more.

I stole a glance in the rearview mirror. The house was a blazing torch in the darkness of the night. I could hear the fierce roaring crackle of the flames over the low growl of the car's engine as a column of smoke rose up through a shower of sparks into the sky. The fire glazed the heavy clouds with a fierce orange glow and lit the road ahead of me for hundreds of yards.

I crunched my foot down hard on the gas pedal and hung a fast turn until I was on the street where Jed and the others would be waiting for me. I saw the silhouette of the house up ahead. I flicked the headlights on and slammed my fist down on the car horn.

I braked hard out front of the house and revved the engine. Exhaust smoke hung heavy on the air, drifting in tendrils past the glaring lights. The street ahead was dark and deserted. I could feel the racing thump of my heart as I snatched expectant anxious glances at the shadowed front door of the house, and then into the rearview mirror.

"Come on!" I growled. I thumped the steering wheel with impatience and then planted my palm down hard on the horn again. "Come on, dammit!" Nothing happened.

I thrust the flashlight through the Yukon's window and aimed the bright beam at the house. The door was still closed, and the house stayed dark and silent as a grave.

Chapter Six.

I counted to five and then swore bitterly. I left the engine running and flung myself out of the Yukon. I ran across the lawn and threw open the front door.

"Jed?" I stormed into the living room, my voice rising in anger and frustration. "Jessica? Where the hell are you?"

I hunted down the hallway and stood for a moment in the kitchen. I was breathing hard. My hands were trembling. I felt a surge of white-hot rage, and it was like a solid lump in my chest.

"Jed!" I called again. I burst into the bedroom growing wild with panic – and froze in the doorway.

Colin Walker was crawling across the floor, propped up on his elbows, his legs dragging heavily behind him, and his face a rictus of horrible pain. There were deep lines of agony cut into his forehead and at the corners of his mouth. His skin was ashen. He was drenched in sweat, the flesh from his forearms raw and bleeding. The bed sheets were tangled like a rope around his ankles from where he had thrown himself from the mattress. He looked up at me and his eyes were black and haunted.

"Jessica," he said. "Your brother took her." The words were torn from him through ragged, exhausted gasps. He rolled onto his back and stared blindly at the ceiling. I dropped to my knees beside him. His chest was heaving, yet each breath was a shallow stab of pain reflected in his eyes.

"Where? Where did he take her?" I asked, not yet realizing the dreadful reality – not yet understanding. "Are they hiding somewhere?"

Walker shook his head and swallowed. "Pentelle," he said. "He left us."

I stared blankly, the monstrous enormity of it dawning slowly through a heavy fog of disbelief. "You mean he kidnapped her?" I gaped at him.

Walker nodded.

I sat back on my haunches and stared dumbly paralyzed with shock. It felt like the walls were closing in on me.

The anger came like a wave, a terrible heaving surge of fierce animal rage, hating Jed for his betrayal with an intensity that staggered me, wanting to thrash and tear at him until his blood splashed and his bones shattered beneath my fists.

"How long ago?" I asked, and there was ice in my voice.

Walker coughed – a wretched sound of pain. "Ten minutes after you left," he said. "Jessica tried to get away from him, but he hit her. He hurt her, Mitch. Then he dragged her by the hair out the front door."

Almost a full hour's head start. It was a lot.

I shook my head. "They left on foot?"

Walker nodded. "To find a car."

There were clothes scattered across the bedroom floor. The wardrobe doors were wide open. I snatched up the first t-shirt I could find and pulled it on. My eyes searched the rest of the room quickly. The nylon bag was missing.

"I tried to stop him…" Walker said weakly. "He took my gun. There was nothing I could do."

I nodded. The pain in his eyes wasn't just physical. He was Secret Service, and he had been unable to protect the person whose safety he was responsible for.

I eased Walker up into a sitting position, with his back propped against a wall, and his legs stretched out in front of him. He clutched at agonizing pain in his chest and blinked away sweat and tears from his eyes.

"I've got a car outside," I said hastily. "But we have to move right now." As I spoke I was hunting through the nearest wardrobe for leather belts. I found two and knelt by his feet. I looked up into Walker's eyes. He was shaking his head mutely.

"I'm going to strap your legs together," I explained. "I think they're broken. But if I can bind them, I can carry you out to the car."

"No…" he flapped his hand in a weak gesture of dismissal. "I can't. I can't make it. Leave me here. Getting Jessica back is all that matters."

I lifted his legs carefully and slid the first belt under his ankles. I tightened the notches until the strap was firm and Walker was biting down hard on his lower lip to stop himself from screaming.

"You're coming with me!" I said. "You can make it!"

He shook his head once more. He seemed to be getting weaker by the minute. I raised his legs again, slid the second belt beneath his knees, and cinched the buckle tight as I dared.

Walker groaned. His breathing was shallow. His head lolled to one side and he stared at me from under heavy drooping eyelids.

"I can't…"

"You can!" I insisted. "I need you, Walker. Jessica needs you."

Precious time was seeping through my fingertips. Every wasted second put Jed and the girl further away – and brought every undead ghoul within a mile inexorably closer. In less than an hour it would be sunrise.

"Okay," Walker said weakly. "But give me your gun. You can't carry me and fight off zombies at the same time. I'll cover us until you get me into the car."

That made sense. I put the old man's gun in his hand and wrapped his fingers around it. He looked down at the weapon, his movements lethargic and uncoordinated. He frowned. "This isn't your gun," he said, turning the weapon over in mild surprise. "It's a Glock 19. Where did you get it?"

"From a dead man," I said grimly, and then explained. "From the man who murdered Clinton Harrigan – the same man I took the car outside from."

The gun hung in Walker's lap. I crouched down to heave him to his feet so that I could carry him, but he held his hand up suddenly. "The water bottle," he pleaded. "It's on the other side of the bed."

I glanced over my shoulder. I couldn't see the water bottle. "I'll find you another one." I said. I was on the verge of panic. It felt like hours had passed since I had discovered Walker, even though in reality it could only have been a few minutes. I imagined the night beyond the house filling with undead as they began to drift away from the burning house in search of fresh prey, and others closer were drawn to the sound of the Yukon's horn and idling engine.

"Please..." Walker pleaded again.

I got to my feet. I was irritated. I hunted round the bed. I pulled at bed sheets, kicked clothes out of the way. I couldn't see the bottle. I dropped to my knees and glared under the mattress.

Then I heard a groan.

I looked up. My eyes went straight to Walker. His head was leaning back against the wall, but his eyes turned in their sockets so that he was looking at me. His mouth was wide open, and the barrel of the Glock was thrust into his mouth.

We stared at each other for just a split-second – long enough for me to realize with horror what he was doing and to understand why, but nowhere near long enough for me to move, or even cry out.

He pulled the trigger, and the bullet blew out through the back of his head, spraying the wall with blood and gore. His body slumped sideways like a falling tree, the gun still gripped in his lifeless hand.

"Christ no!" I swore in the agony of bitter frustration. But I didn't scramble to Walker's aid. There was no point. He was dead, and there was nothing I could do. I stood over his body, paralyzed for more seconds than I could spare, and then I went down on my haunches and gently prized the gun from his fingers while fresh blood pumped from the wound and seeped into the carpet around my feet.

Walker had sacrificed his life to buy me time – time to escape in the Yukon to pursue Jed and the girl. He knew the gunshot and blood would draw the undead to the house. I dared not waste what small chance he had given his life for.

I ran through the house, back out through the front door. I paused on the grassy shoulder of the road for a split second and cast my eyes towards the east. The night sky was lightening – the faintest, softest glow of a new day about to dawn through a veil of dark purple clouds.

All around me, the night seemed to be alive with dangerous movement and sound. I saw drifting shapes like ghostly apparitions appear at the end of the road, and then I heard a sudden snarling growl from over my shoulder. I spun on my heel and threw the Glock up in an action that was purely reflex. A figure lunged for me – the body of a huge fat man, its skin withered and dry, its features desiccated and shriveled. The sound in the ghoul's throat became a keening wail of triumph. It was so close – towering over me like an avalanche of rage – close enough to smell the rank fetid stench of its breath and hear the hiss of air across its throat. At the last possible second I pulled the trigger and the recoil of the gun was like a liquid pulse that jolted up through my hand and the muzzle blast beat thunderously against my ears.

The shot tore a ragged hole in the ghoul's forehead and punched it backwards into the grass.

I swung the gun in an arc. Behind the zombie was another figure, its body spasming as it burst from behind a dense garden bush. It had been a woman. Now it was a shriveled emaciated ghoul with a wiry tangle of black hair, its arms and legs thin as sticks, its skin dry and dusty as parchment. I fired twice. The first bullet missed completely. I heard it ricochet away into the night. The second shot hit the zombie in the shoulder and flung it round in a tight circle. It teetered like that for an instant and then dropped to its knees, glaring hatefully over its shoulder at me, still snarling with venom.

I couldn't waste another shot. I ran for the Yukon and flung myself behind the wheel. I stamped my foot on the gas and the car leaped forward, racing towards the sunrise – racing towards the Interstate in pursuit of Jed.

The clock was ticking in my head again, but it was no longer counting the passage of elapsed time – it was counting down like a time bomb.

Chapter Seven.

I drove east for a couple of miles, with my foot flat down on the gas pedal, hunched over the steering wheel and taking the corners with reckless desperation. The suburban streets were littered with abandoned cars and strewn with garbage. There were station wagons still in their driveways, their roof-racks piled high with camping gear and household possessions, and there were overturned wrecked vehicles, blackened and burned, or crumpled from collisions. And laying like litter on the streets were the bodies of those who had been savaged by the undead, tattered and dismembered, left out in the sun for the crows and rats to feast upon the carcasses.

I swerved and weaved around the strewn wreckage and the Yukon's big tires screeched in protest until I came to an intersection where three cars had been rammed by an out-of control truck.

Suddenly I had to slow, and the initial surge of panic in me abated. I knew that Jed had an hour head start, but I also realized I couldn't catch him if I wrecked the Yukon, or sent it careering off the hazard-strewn road. I eased off the gas and swung the Yukon through the crash site, my feet dancing between the pedals until I had the Yukon up on the sidewalk and then jolting back down onto the blacktop with clear road stretched out ahead of me.

I cut my speed to twenty and concentrated on casting my eyes well ahead for signs of trouble or danger. It felt like I was crawling – it felt like I was losing time, but I resisted the urge to risk accelerating.

I passed an intersection and then found myself driving into a messy tangle of streets that crouched ahead of me. It was a sprawling housing project, spread to the north and the west. There was a ragged little cluster of dark mean storefronts with their windows smashed. A couple of the buildings had been burned out and there were upended shopping trolleys on the sidewalk around a corner grocery store that had been looted. I drove past squat, dark brick buildings with narrow windows and past parking lots sprinkled with abandoned cars, their paintwork dewed with overnight rain. There was a basketball court, fenced in by high chain link and surrounded by brick walls sprayed with frantic graffiti.

The morning was silent. The air was hot and damp. I wound down the driver's side window, but the air was heavy with the putrid stench of rotting decay. Crows took to angry flight squawking in belligerent protest as I drove past, and then swooped down again to resume picking at the bodies.

Over my shoulder, dawn was coming on quickly, the sun rising in the east behind banks of purple and grey clouds that were stacking up on the horizon. The sky changed to orange and the narrow streets filled with long uncertain shadows as the sun's tentative light signaled a new day.

The edge of the housing estate was marked by a couple of vacant lots overgrown with grass and bordered by low wire fencing, and then a gas station with a couple of weary pumps out front and windows that had been boarded over.

I drove on past an old billboard and then a bar. The back of the bar was filled with wooden crates and metal beer kegs that lay scattered on their side like knocked down bowling pins. There were a couple of big trash receptacles in the parking lot and an old rusted out Chevy with blocks of timber under its brake drums.

I cruised by slowly and then saw a tin sign on a post on the sidewalk, faded and pock-marked with rusty spots, pointing the way to the I-64. It was shaped like a shield, painted red and blue, with an arrow pointing left beneath it. I reached the next cross-street and swung the Yukon onto a wide stretch of level flat road – and had to slam down hard on the brakes.

There was a black and white Crown Vic cop car slewed across the road, its nose in the gutter. The driver's door was open. On the blacktop beside the vehicle were the remains of a police officer; his tan jacket torn to shreds. One of his shoes was a dozen feet away, the severed foot protruding from the leather. There was pump action riot gun on the road, and a mange-riddled black dog was standing over the body, gnawing on a bone. The dog looked up at the sound of the Yukon braking and it stared at me through the windshield with rabid wild eyes, its head sinking low between its shoulders as it growled.

Beyond the cop car was a green compact. The front end of the little car had been shunted into a telegraph pole and the driver's side of the vehicle was a mess of crumpled sheet metal. The windshield was shattered. There was broken glass sprayed across the hood of the car, shining in the sunlight like a thousand diamonds. The driver of the compact had been hurled head-first through the glass and his body lay sprawled across the bonnet. In his dead hand was a small black pistol.

I could guess the tale of the tragedy by what was written in the bloody footprints that spread in confused patterns across the road and in the trampled grass beyond. I could imagine the cop running the compact off the road and the impact as the little car went head-first into the power pole. Maybe the cop had been injured – maybe shot in the seconds before the collision by the driver – and he had dragged himself from the cop car bleeding from his wounds and drawn the riot gun from between the seats. There were empty shell casings laying in the gutter where the officer had opened fire before being overwhelmed by undead ghouls that had spilled from the surrounding buildings and torn his body to shreds.

The blood was dry, the cop car covered in a fine layer of dust.

I glanced to the buildings on both side of the road, suddenly overcome with the sensation that I was being watched. I felt my skin crawl with eerie dread. The buildings on either side seemed to hunch over me as I nosed the Yukon up over the curb and onto the grassy shoulder. The big tires gouged into the soft ground and the suspension swayed as I crawled around the wreckage and then dropped back onto the blacktop. I stabbed my foot down on the gas and the Yukon seemed to leap forward with relief.

The buildings became low rise and spaced further apart, then became lonely farmsteads scattered on the side of the road behind clusters of mailboxes. I drove for a couple of minutes and covered a couple more miles, then rode down a slight hill and back up again. There were more buildings in the distance, all of them built low to the ground, lit up from behind by the morning sun.

I drove by another roadside sign for the Interstate, and then I was cruising past a diner and a Texaco gas station with a mechanic's workshop attached. There was a dented and dusty pick up truck parked out front of the diner. It looked like some kind of a farm truck.

I slowed to a crawl as I passed. The diner looked like the kind of place the local cops would stop for their morning coffee and doughnuts. There was a flat area of beaten down earth alongside the building with a couple of abandoned cars parked on the shoulder of the road. I glanced back through the windshield – and then a flash of wild movement caught the corner of my eye and the sound of a door slamming tore the silence apart. My head snapped round. There was a woman lurching towards the side of the road. She had burst through the front door of the diner. Behind her loomed a dozen dark shapes, swarming out into the bright sunlight, snarling with maddened rage.

I slammed my foot on the brake. The Yukon dipped low at the nose and then lurched to a stop on squealing brakes. The woman was hobbling towards me, dragging one of her legs behind her, limp and crippled. She was young, her face a white mask of terror. She flailed her arms at me, shrieking for help, and I noticed there was blood at the corner of her mouth, spilling down her chin.

I snatched up the Glock from the seat beside me and thrust the gun out through the window, aiming past the running woman at the undead. They were convulsing and writhing as they hunted her, cutting down the distance between them and their prey, and moving with alarming speed.

"Come on!" I shouted.

The woman was sobbing, her mouth twisted into a grimace of pain and desperation, her eyes huge. She wrenched her head round and glanced over her shoulder then screamed aloud. The nearest zombie was just a few feet away. It lunged for her with its fingers seized into claws, but the girl rolled her shoulder at the last possible second and the ghoul's fingernails tangled in the fabric of her blouse. She tore herself free, but she was weakening now. Her next steps were exhausted and slow, her legs uncertain beneath her. She was gasping for breath. She turned back to me, her expression desperate and imploring. I fired into the mass of undead and one of the ghouls staggered and then dropped to its knees but the others swept past and the sound of their voices rose to a clamorous evil roar.

I fired again and kicked my door open. I fired twice more with a double-fisted grip, and the recoil of the Glock slammed up through my arms to my shoulders. One of the shots went wide and the other hit an undead woman in the chest and knocked her stumbling to the ground. "Come on!" I screamed hoarsely. "You can make it! Keep running!"

I thrust out my free hand – urging the woman on. She reached out towards me, her fingertips tantalizingly close... and then one of the zombies caught hold of her hair and reefed her off her feet. The woman was flung savagely backwards like she had been struck full in the chest by the blast of a shotgun. She landed on her back in the middle of the road, and within an instant the undead were swarming over her body. I heard the woman cry out once – a blood-curdling scream of agony and terror – before I let my foot slide off the brake and mash the gas pedal to the floorboards. The Yukon tore away in a screech of blue smoke and I had to throw down the Glock and snatch at the wheel to keep the car on the road. I got a hundred yards clear and slammed the car's door shut, then braked again, keeping the engine revving high.

In the rearview mirror I could see the undead dismembering the woman, fighting over the scraps of her flesh like vicious animals, their bodies drenched in her blood as the corpse was torn to pieces. Her head rolled across the road into the gutter. One of the undead scurried after it and was instantly set upon by the others.

I drove away slowly, shaken and sickened. I was numb, my mind replaying the dreadful few seconds, haunted by the helpless panic in the woman's eyes at the instant she had been snatched away from me. I might have covered another mile or two before I suddenly realized the blacktop had become wider and then went into a slow turning rise with iron guardrails posted on both sides. I gave the Yukon some gas and crested the on-ramp doing thirty, with the four wide lanes of the I-64 suddenly stretched out before me.

I hung in the merge lane and touched the brakes until the Yukon was just crawling. The interstate ran straight as an arrow into the distance. About a hundred yards ahead was a framework of high girders mounted with huge green directional signs, listing the oncoming towns. I ran my eyes quickly down the list. Pentelle was 23 miles away – I figured that meant about twenty miles of interstate before I had to look for the off-ramp.

Nothing moved on the road. Nothing at all. The sun had burned away the early morning clouds and now the heat beat through the windshield so that I felt a prickle of sweat down my back. I swung the Yukon into the nearest lane and gradually built up speed.

The silence was eerie. There were abandoned cars in every lane, doors left open, the contents of the vehicles scattered like debris. It was like some dreadful battle scene – as if the air force had overflown the freeway and strafed the torrent of refugees fleeing east. The road's surface was gouged and stained with leaked oil and spilled blood. I saw bodies scattered amongst the wreckage, but not many.

I nudged the Yukon up to thirty-five then forty. On the wide open expanse of the freeway I felt more confident. Navigating the wreckage of abandoned cars was like steering a slalom course but visibility was good: the road was flat and straight and I had a clear view of what lay ahead well before I needed to take evasive action. The miles slid slowly by, and as I scanned the horizon my thoughts drifted to Jed and the girl, Jessica.

Walker said Jed had hurt the girl. How badly?

He was a brutal callous man, and I knew he was capable of anything – even murder. But I also knew he was cunning and resourceful. He was making a run for Pentelle, but he wasn't doing it out of honor or because the Vice President's teenage daughter was at risk. He was doing it to save his life – to barter her safety for his own. In doing so he had forsaken Colin Walker and abandoned me.

Leaving me for dead I could understand. He had sworn he would kill me for the death of his wife and child. If he couldn't kill me – then leaving me to die at the hands of the undead would be just as effective, if not as satisfying.

Walker was Secret Service, and he had lied to us from the moment we had pulled him and the girl from the wrecked helicopter. In Jed's mind, that most likely justified the slow painful death he had condemned the man to.

I drove on until I passed beneath another green traffic billboard, with arrows pointing to an off-ramp and the name of the nearby towns written in big white letters. I glanced up at the sign.

Pentelle: 12 miles.

I flexed my fingers on the steering wheel. It was mid-morning. The sun was blazing through the windshield, and the early morning overcast had given way to a blue cloudless sky. On the side of the road grew dense thickets of trees and the freeway began to undulate up crests and then down into gentle green valleys.

I edged the Yukon up to forty-five and swept around a long gentle curve as the road cut a path between two grassy wooded slopes.

The Yukon came out of the curve and I touched the brakes cautiously. I was in one of the middle lanes, and up ahead, at the top of a gentle crest, I could see the debris of several cars and a truck, stretched across the road.

A mile out I cut my speed to twenty. The road looked completely blocked. The truck was overturned on its side and slewed across two lanes. It had been carrying a load of scrap metal. The blacktop was cluttered with twisted pieces of iron and broken glass. There was a body of a man nearby, laying flat on its back. Crows were perched on the bloated stomach, feasting on the remains. Near the rear of the truck was a little red Japanese hatch. The front of the car had been completely crushed when it had been side-swiped by the out–of-control truck. The car sat hard down at the nose with both its front wheels broken from the axle. The passenger-side door of the hatch was open and there was a trail of thick swerving skid-marks burned onto the blacktop.

I cut my speed to ten, the Yukon barely creeping forward, and I hunched over the steering wheel feeling a sudden cold hand of despair clutch at my heart and wring the last glimmers of hope from me.

Parked up against the waist-high concrete Jersey barrier that divided the east and westbound lanes was a grey Ford Taurus. The car looked old and grimy. It looked like it was wedged between the wreckage of the red hatchback and the concrete deflector, like maybe it had tried to burrow through the narrow gap and become jammed. Both the driver's side doors were wide open, and there was a body lying out on the road near the rear wheel. I crept closer, cursing bitterly under my breath. I considered backing up all the way to the off-ramp – but it was miles behind me and I knew if I did that I would never reach Pentelle.

I threw the transmission into neutral and sat fuming while the big Yukon's engine softly gurgled and bubbled. There was a gap between the front-end of the crushed compact and the tail of the truck – but not wide enough for me to drive through without risking serious damage to the Yukon. I glanced over my shoulder: the forest pressed close to the side of the road, dense and impenetrable.

I stared hard at the fringe of undergrowth, and at that instant an unexpected movement caught my eye. It was the body lying by the wheel of the Taurus.

I saw it move.

It was a man. He was laying on his side, with one arm thrown over his face and the other close to his body. I saw the man's hand move, and realized too late that it was clutching a gun.

Time seemed to stand still.

I saw the man begin to roll his body, his arm coming away from his face as he pushed himself up onto his knees. I heard the Yukon's engine roar like a wounded beast as I slammed the selector into 'Drive' and crushed my foot down hard on the gas. I saw the man with the gun raise his arm, swinging it in a fluid arc until I was looking down the barrel.

I saw the man's face.

It was Jed.

The Yukon raced towards the tail of the overturned truck, swinging like a scythe as I fought to steady the wheel. I wrenched it over at the last moment and there was a flash of red across the windshield as the little compact disappeared under the nose of the Yukon and then the sound of a tremendous metallic bang that punched me forward against the steering wheel. Sheet metal tore and I was thrown violently against the door. My head cannoned forward then bounced back into the headrest as my hands were wrenched from the wheel and the car burst through the narrow gap, shunting the compact round in a crackle and shriek of metal that jarred my teeth.

The tinted rear window suddenly exploded. I lifted my foot off the gas and tapped the brakes, then spun the wheel in a hard lock to the right. The Yukon swished her big cumbersome tail in a screech of blue smoke and went into a slide. But I was going too fast, the vehicle still swaying and rocking on spongy springs. She went up onto the off-side wheels. I had a split second to cry out in alarm and panic – and then the car rolled over onto its side.

I was thrown across the cabin as the car slewed in a shower of sparks and thunderous noise. I felt my head crack against something hard and heavy, and for an instant everything went black. I blinked. I was bleeding – blood trickling from a gash in my scalp and running down my face.

My head was pounding. The cabin filled with dust and smoke. Through the singing in my ears I heard another gunshot and an instant later the ricochet as the bullet zinged away into the distant morning sky.

I fumbled frantically for the Glock. It was wedged under the seat that had been wrenched off its runners and jammed against the door of the car by the impact. I clawed at the weapon and tugged it free, then braced my back and kicked the windshield out.

I stumbled from the wreckage and my legs collapsed from beneath me. I went down on the sun-baked tarmac, sagging to my knees. I slumped against the hissing grille of the Yukon, and dragged myself around until I had the vehicle between myself and the roadblock.

Another shot ripped through the still morning air and I flinched instinctively. A flash of metallic sparks was torn from the fender, not a foot from my head. I tucked myself into a ball. My hands were shaking, yet my mind was suddenly very clear, the reality very certain.

I was going to die.

I rolled my shoulders and stole a glance back along the freeway. I could see Jed, leaning over the hood of the red hatchback with the Glock in both hands, his arms braced to steady his aim. He was firing from just fifty feet away – firing from the crest of the rise. It was only a matter of time.

I turned and stared ahead into the distance. The road fell away in a gradual slope for another wreckage-strewn mile, and then flattened out and widened into an extra lane in the shadow of a freeway overpass.

The off-ramp to Pentelle.

It was so close, yet impossibly far away.

In desperation, I glanced sideways to the fringe of dense trees. I narrowed my eyes, judging the distance. They were about thirty feet away, across two lanes of open road and a narrow belt of dry tufted grass. The woods were deeply shadowed and thick with scrubby undergrowth. I screwed my eyes shut and took a deep breath.

"I knew you'd follow me, fucker!" I heard Jed shout clearly in the stillness. "I knew you'd come after the girl. You're a dead man!"

I said nothing. I felt my heart beating like it wanted to break out through my chest, and an uncomfortable warm wetness across the front of my shirt that puzzled me. I checked the Glock had a round in the chamber and heaved myself into a crouch. My hands felt numb, my fingers swollen. I glanced down and realized the top of my little finger of my left hand had been severed below the first knuckle. Blood was oozing from the wound, the shock deadening the pain of the injury. I ripped my t-shirt open and used the long shreds to bind the stump and then used my teeth to pull the knot tight.

"You're insane, Jed!" I shouted out, buying myself a few precious seconds of time. "You've got a head full of faulty wiring. You're a murderer!"

There was an eerie silence and I used those moments to brace my back against the grille, ready to push off hard and make a desperate dash for the tree line.

Thirty feet. The distance suddenly telescoped out before me and looked like a million miles. I knew I wouldn't make it.

"What did you say?" Jed snapped hotly.

"I said you're fucked up in the head!" I shouted back. There was another impossibly long silence – suspiciously long. I stole another glance around the edge of the Yukon.

Jed was gone.

Three shots suddenly rang out, three viciously loud retorts, and the air erupted around me. I flinched away, covered my head with my hands, and realized that Jed had crept around behind the Taurus and then climbed over the Jersey barrier to outflank me from the middle of the road. The bullets ripped into the grille, just inches from my head and shoulders.

I sprang to my feet and fled towards the trees, weaving and jinking my body, running doubled-over at the waist with the blood pounding in my ears and every step on trembling fear-filled legs.

Instantly the air around me erupted, hot against my cheek, buffeting me with the whiplash of gunfire.

I wasn't going to make it.

I reached the shoulder of the road. My feet crunched over loose gravel and then I hit the narrow belt of long stringy grass that grew in brown ragged tufts along the verge. I lifted my legs high, like I was running into a foaming ocean of breaking surf.

Ten more feet.

I ran with my jaw clenched tight, anticipating the next shot, the muscles in my back seized, awaiting the bullet that would knock me down.

It had to come.

It had to come now.

I threw myself down into the grass. I hit the ground with such violence that the air was punched from my lungs. My teeth slammed together and I tasted the coppery tang of blood in my mouth. I rolled over, and then suddenly plunged into a narrow drainage ditch as bullets thrashed and beat at the grass with a sound like a bullwhip.

I groaned. I was laying face down in a trench, like a shallow grave. The ground beneath me was muddy red clay. The trench was as wide as my shoulders and I edged my body round until I was lying on my side, gasping raggedly as I tried to suck in lungsful of air and stop myself from shaking. Sweat and blood trickled into my eyes. I scraped my hand down my face and wiped it on the tatters of my shirt, then slowly inched my head above the height of the drainage ditch.

Through the long grass I could see Jed. He was kneeling behind the Jersey barrier with a clear shot to where I had fallen. He had the Glock held in a double-fisted grip. He was waiting.

I moved in inches, ever so slowly raising the gun and aiming for the small blob of Jed's head through the untamed tufted blades of grass. It was an awkward position for I had no way to support my head to sight the weapon without presenting myself as a target.

I squeezed the trigger – a one-in-a-million shot – and saw the bullet strike the concrete barrier about ten feet to Jed's left.

"Fucker!" Jed threw back his head and laughed out loud. "Is that the best you've got?" he mocked me, shouting in rage and hatred. He opened fire and the grass around me was thrashed by the pass of shot. I ducked my head – buried the side of my face down in the damp mud and counted to five.

"I should never have trusted my baby girl to you," Jed shouted from the middle of the road. "I should never have relied on you to protect my wife. You're not man enough – you never were!" his voice was enraged.

I was pinned down. Trapped. I knew if I got to my feet and tried to reach the line of the trees, Jed wouldn't miss.

It was hopeless.

"Susie wasn't your child, Jed," I cried out. "She was mine. She was my child, and Debbie was my woman." Suddenly I couldn't stop the words. Suddenly it didn't seem to matter any more. I had to tell him now. "We were in love. Your wife was leaving you, Jed. She was coming with me," I shouted. "That's why I picked you up from the bus station. I was driving you back so we could tell you."

There was a deathly silence – a silence that was heavy with monstrous shock. It lasted a full minute and there was not a sound in the world.

"You're... you're lying!" Jed roared. "You're a fuckin' liar!"

"No. I'm not." I stood up, knee-deep in the ditch. I got to my feet slowly, my hands by my side and I was dizzy and swaying. My chest burned, and the pain in my left hand was a fierce throb – but I was calm and without fear for the first time in weeks.

"No, Jed," I said, and there was regret and sadness in my voice. "I'm not lying. Susie was my daughter, not yours."

I stared across the open ground, past the wreckage of the Yukon to where my brother was rising from behind the Jersey barrier. He was shaking his head in incredulous disbelief, and I saw the Glock in his hand waver.

"Debbie...?"

I nodded. We were about thirty feet apart. Too far for him to see the sadness in my eyes, too far to hear the heavy tone of my voice. The pain of losing her still ached within me like an open wound that would never heal. "We never meant for it to happen, Jed. We never meant to fall in love..."

Jed turned away, then spun back suddenly. The gun came up, aimed squarely at my chest. "No," he moaned. "No." The Glock wobbled in his hand, then steadied. He glared over the weapon at me, his face cold and brutal and merciless. And then his hand fell to his side and he bent over at the waist like he was in physical pain. "No!" he roared.

I stood there. I didn't move.

Jed snapped upright and his arm shot out, the gun in his fist. There was murder in his eyes.

"I'm sorry," I said. "I've carried this secret for years," I went on, shaking my head with regret.

Jed's gaze went dead, and the rage within him finally erupted. "Now you'll take it to your grave!" he roared.

He pulled the trigger, and I felt the bullet punch me hard in the chest, a little off center, with a force like a sledge-hammer. The impact hurled me round and I staggered backwards. I clutched at the pain – clamped my hand over the wound – and tumbled backwards into the long grass.

I stared up at the blue sky. The sun was high, winking through the fringe of leafy green treetops. I blinked my eyes. My throat felt closed and my tongue seemed to fill my mouth – but for all that there was no pain. I felt numb, and there was a cold chill seeping through my veins. I turned my head and saw Jed striding across the freeway, gun swinging from his hand, his steps purposeful and determined. His silhouette bounced and wavered and then he was standing over me, blocking out the sun with the broad of his back so that my face was cast in shadow.

I blinked again. My vision darkened, then came back. I licked my lips and tasted blood on my tongue. My skin felt like it was burning.

Jed's shape wavered and then came back into focus. My vision began to blur and mist, and the silence was filled with a loud humming sound like a garden of angry bees.

I was laying flat on my back, arms out flung, the Glock somehow still in my stiffened hand.

Jed glowered down at me. "I hope it fuckin' hurts!" he spat.

I opened my mouth to speak but the words were just an inaudible husky whisper. I could feel the ragged tear in my shirt, along the ridge of my pectoral muscle and welling blood oozing like treacle through my fingers.

Jed crouched down on his haunches. "Got something to say?" his voice was cruel. "Another death-bed confession?"

I swallowed hard. My mouth was dry, my lips felt thick and swollen. The taste of blood was stronger. I coughed, a spasm of pain that racked me, and turned my head until I was staring into Jed's brutal eyes.

"The girl?" I croaked.

"Which one?" Jed growled. "My wife you were screwing, my daughter you took from me – or the Vice President's snotty little bitch?"

I closed my eyes as a sudden lance of pain ripped through my chest like a stabbing red-hot poker. "Jessica."

"She's in the trunk," he said. "The little bitch is a fireball. I had to slap her around to keep her quiet," he admitted with rueful delight. "But she's alive. She needs to be right? She's my meal ticket out of this Hell and back to civilization."

I felt a sick, helpless flutter of revulsion. "Civilization would be better off without you," I rasped.

Jed's temper flared. He pressed the gun against my forehead. I felt the steel of the barrel. It was warm. I felt the pressure of it against my skin. I took a shallow breath, and then my face twisted in the pain of sudden effort, as I summoned the very last reserves of my strength.

Jed frowned down at me thoughtfully. Then he snatched the gun away from my forehead and leaned closer, pressing his face close to mine, so that his words were ragged and harsh and loud in my ear. "I've decided to let you bleed out," he said maliciously. "I'm not giving you a quick death, fucker. You're not worth another bullet. If the zombies don't get you, the ants will – or the crows…"

He started to rise, and as he got back to his haunches he realized too late that I had hefted the Glock in my out flung hand. I held my breath, groaned with the effort – and squeezed the trigger with the last trembling ounces of my strength. The bullet caught Jed in the side of his neck, and tore out through the other side of his head in a pink eruption of blood and a thunderous roar. The recoil slammed my hand back into the grass and then an instant later I saw my brother's astonished lifeless eyes, as he toppled into the grass beside me.

He was dead.

* * *

I closed my eyes and lay still for a long time, feeling the waves of pain rippling through my chest, growing stronger and more violent until I was writhing through gritted teeth and a groan of agony was ripped from my throat.

Something nearby moved, padded away. I didn't care.

Then I heard the growl and whine of a dog. I opened my eyes and rolled onto my side. The German Shepherd was fifteen feet away, watching me hungrily from the line of the trees. Its eyes were fixed. Its mouth hung open, thick ropes of saliva drooling from its slack jaw. The dog snarled at me.

It looked sick. Its fur was hanging from its scrawny body in clumps, its legs stained in dry blood. It rocked its head from side to side and took a cautious step forward, slipping out of the shadowed woods and into the sunlight.

The animal stank; a putrid smell of rotting decay and death. It bared its teeth at me and they were yellow and wicked as razors.

I felt for the gun. It was still in my hand, but my arm was numb so that it dragged limp across the ground and I could not bring the weapon to bare.

The German Shepherd trotted in a wide wary circle around me, its eyes never leaving mine, until it was between my body and the freeway. I tried to shout, but my voice was nothing more than a weary croak. There was a froth of bubbles at the corner of my mouth. I heaved myself upright and screamed out in pain at the effort.

The German Shepherd scampered away, then crept back until it was just ten feet away. It growled, and its eyes looked maddened with desperate hunger and starvation.

Its long pink tongue lolled from the side of its mouth and then it suddenly sniffed harshly like it could taste the scent of my blood on the air. The dog's head sank low on its shoulders and it took three bold paces towards my legs.

I tried to raise the gun, willed it to move, frowning with the intense desperate effort of concentration, but my arm hung heavy in the grass and would not move. I reached across myself and snatched up the Glock into my left hand. It was shaking and unsteady. The weapon wavered. I closed one eye to focus, but my vision flared into an explosion of white bursting light and I groaned in weakened pain.

I fired into the air and the dog fled across two lanes of the road, growling and yelping in confused terror, then turned back, suddenly more cautious, yet overcome by the ferocity of its hunger.

It slinked to the edge of the grass and went down on its haunches, creeping forward in stealthy inches. I raised the gun again in my left hand, but the weight of the weapon was impossibly heavy, my fingers slick with my own blood. I felt the gun slip from my grip and I could not pick it up again.

The German Shepherd raised its head and we stared at each other across the small space. Its ears flattened against its head and it came up from the ground onto its haunches, tensed like a spring. The dog's jaw hung slack – and then it lunged.

I screamed until the pain in my chest left me dizzy, yet made no sound louder than a ragged croak. The dog's fierce teeth latched into flesh, just below the knee and it snarled ferocious and wide eyed with frenzy and madness. I beat my fist on the grass, but it was useless.

The German Shepherd clamped its jaws into fleshy muscle and began to drag at Jed's dead body, worrying its teeth and rolling its head from side to side, growling and snarling.

In desperation and horror I reached across my body and picked up the Glock in my right hand. I had no feeling – no sensation other than pain. The arm was heavy as lead and I had to hold it steady with my blood-covered left hand bracing the elbow.

I fired at the dog and hit it in the rump. The animal shrieked in terrible pain and let go of Jed's leg. It went over in the grass, thrashing and yelping. I fired again – a gut shot – and the terrible noise was cut off abruptly.

I looked about me dazedly. I was drenched in blood. It soaked through my shirt and welled in my lap. It mingled with Jed's blood and that of the dog, and soaked into the grassy earth.

Eventually the undead would come. Maybe it would take another hour – maybe another day. But I knew sooner or later one would pick up the scent and follow it to my body.

I stared up at the sky. Was this how it was meant to end?

Was I meant to merely bleed to death in the dirt?

Was Jessica Steinman meant to suffocate in the trunk of a car?

Or was I meant to die trying?

I tucked the gun into the blood-soaked waistband of my jeans. I closed my eyes and dug down for every last scrap of strength. With a terrible pain-filled heave, I got to my knees. I felt myself trembling. I felt the agony of every ragged breath. I closed my eyes again and saw bright flashing lights of color. I bit down on my lip to stifle a scream, and heaved myself to my feet. My knees went from beneath me and I swayed perilously, like a drunken man.

"Jessica!" I called, the words not more than a hoarse rasp across my throat. I lurched and staggered towards the freeway.

The sun beat down on me, and the singing in my ears rose to a deafening crescendo. I felt my blood, warm against my skin, as it spilled down my waist and left a crimson spattered trail across the burning blacktop.

I reached the wrecked Yukon and clutched at it to support my weight. I was slick with sweat and blood, and I heard myself making small mewing whimpering sounds as the tide of agony swept over me and crashed through my body in a torrent of pain. I looked over my shoulder, my eyes dazedly following the dipping freeway to where it flattened beneath the overpass, and to where I knew the off-ramp sign to Pentelle was, but the image wavered and rippled like I was peering through a heat-hazed mirage.

I turned my head slowly and looked to where the Taurus was wedged against the concrete barrier. It was fifty feet up a gentle slope to the crest of the rise, but it stretched before me like the peak of Everest.

I pushed myself away from the Yukon, took two tottering steps, and then got my balance. I staggered, clutching at my chest like a man in the grips of a heart attack, while every effort and every pace cost me blood and strength.

I knew I couldn't keep going.

I slumped to my knees and began to crawl.

When I reached the Taurus I was trembling like a man in fever. My skin burned, my arm was stiff and limp. I fumbled for the trunk lever down by the driver's seat and it was like trying to lift a mighty weight. I grimaced, felt my teeth bite through my bottom lip, and then I heard the soft echoing sound of the catch releasing. I rolled onto my back, panting with exhaustion, and let the waves of agony wash me away into the sweet oblivion of darkness.

* * *

"Get up! Jesus Christ, please get up!"

I tried to push the tugging hands away, unwilling to come back from the comfortable respite of unconsciousness, but the voice was strident and relentless, the hands that shook me desperate.

I opened my eyes. They were heavy, and felt crusted with grit. I blinked, and my head lolled to the side. I felt hands beneath my armpits, trying to lift me, and I groaned in pain until the piercing agony of being moved brought me to wakefulness.

Jessica Steinman's face hovered over me, its edges blurred. I blinked my eyes until they focused, and saw the deep fearful lines of panic cut into her brow.

Her face was swollen, and there was a livid red bruise on her cheek, already beginning to darken purple.

"Stay with me," she said, her voice trembling. "Don't die on me."

I was propped up against the side of the car, shaded from the sun by the wreckage of the truck. I flapped my hand feebly, and tried to tell her everything was all right. I wanted her to know that the pain wasn't so bad any more. I wanted her to know that I had tried… but no sound came from my mouth.

"I've pressed the beacon," Jessica said, holding up her arm and shaking the bracelet around her wrist. "I've been pressing it every few seconds for the past ten minutes," her voice was fraught and pleading. "Just stay with me a little longer. There must be a helicopter on its way."

I shook my head. It felt as heavy as a cannonball upon my shoulders. I took a shallow breath and licked my lips. My mouth was dry. "Still twelve miles," I said in a raw husky whisper. "Still too far…"

I saw her turn her head and stare for long seconds, as though maybe she heard a sound, or maybe she saw something. When she turned back to me her face was suddenly pale and grey as ash.

"Zombies?" I croaked.

She nodded, not trusting her voice. Her eyes were enormous, like she was on the edge of sheer terror.

"Where?"

"They're... they're back down the road, coming from the west," she said.

"Coming this way?"

She nodded and trapped her lip between her teeth with panic. "About a dozen of them."

I groaned. I tried to heave myself upright but I didn't have the strength. I coughed, and a splash of bright red blood trickled down my chin. "Go," I wheezed. "Run for it."

She shook her head vehemently. "No!"

I lay there panting in short shallow breaths through sickening waves of nausea and moments where the darkness came and then receded again. My mind was numb, my thoughts confused and chittering. I frowned and tried to find a way...

"The car," I said.

Jessica shook her head. "I think it broke down. He couldn't get it to start. I heard him trying. I thought he'd left me in the trunk to die."

"Get in," I said again. "Let the brake off. You'll roll down the hill."

She understood instantly. With the Taurus parked on the crest of the rise it would only take momentum to send it rolling down the gentle slope, carrying her at least to the Pentelle turnoff and to safety. She glanced quickly over her shoulder and gave a little gasp of dread, but her expression stayed grim with determination.

"You too," she insisted. She got behind me and tried to lift me into the passenger seat of the car. I shook my head, groaning and weak, but she got her hands under my armpits and cried out with the effort. Blood spilled across the blacktop and across the car seat. I slumped heavily and heard the door slam.

Jessica flung herself behind the wheel and scraped her tangled hair back from her face. She was breathing hard, like she was on the verge of hyperventilating. I saw her glance up into the rear view mirror and shriek.

She slipped the handbrake and the Taurus began to inch forward, the tires crunching over broken glass. She clung to the steering wheel with white knuckles, her eyes darting from the mirrors to the road ahead and then back again. The car picked up speed, slowly gaining momentum until we rolled past the wrecked Yukon. I saw dark flashes loom up beside the car. I heard heavy thumps beat upon the panels. I heard Jessica scream – and then suddenly all was silent but for the sound of the car's tires whispering across the blacktop.

We rolled to the bottom of the slope and Jessica got the car into the off-ramp lane, turning the wheel in short anxious jerks until she had the vehicle lined up with the bend. The speed of the Taurus bled away, carrying us into the turn and down the ramp before rolling to a halt on a narrow tree-lined stretch of road.

Jessica slumped back in the driver's seat and gave a ragged shaky gasp of relief. She turned to me, and I felt the tender touch of her hand, trembling, but warm on my cheek. I forced my eyes to focus, blinking through a fog of pain – and saw her thrust her head suddenly forward, tense and alert, staring up through the windshield as she frantically hunted the sky.

I barely noticed. I could feel death's hand reaching out for me; feel the whisper touch of its fingertips begin to squeeze the last ounces of life from within. I took a long deep breath, and felt something deep inside my chest tear. My ears were ringing and then the noise became a loud thumping drone – a sound I couldn't clear. I squeezed my eyes tightly shut, and when I opened them again, the sound had become a beating roar.

I slumped back in the seat, and shook my head.

Jessica was smiling at me, her mouth forming words I couldn't hear, and couldn't understand. She pointed out through the windshield and her eyes filled with joyous tears that streamed down the swelling of her bruised cheek. She clapped her hands together and then covered her mouth as though muttering some silent prayer of relief and gratitude.

I turned my head. A helicopter hung just inches above the road, settling down on its wide skids amidst a haze of dust and debris that filled the air like a sandstorm. I saw the word 'Navy' near the tail rotor and a big blue roundel inset with the white star painted on the fuselage, before three dark bulky shapes spilled from the open doorway. Two of the men ran to the rear of the car, carrying weapons held high across their chests, their faces dour and tense. The third man ran directly towards the vehicle.

I drifted in and out of darkness. Howling wind whipped and shredded the trees, and the air filled with dust that was hurled across the windshield with the sound like horizontal rain.

I heard more noise, suddenly louder, and a rush of wind swirled in through the driver's side door. I rolled my head slowly to the side and saw a man wearing a heavy helmet with a microphone obscuring his mouth. The man had calm steady eyes. He was hunched in through the doorway, his face pressed close to Jessica's. He was clutching a piece of white plastic, the size of a paperback book.

"Name?" the man had to shout above the percussive thump of the helicopter's rotors.

"Jessica Margaret Steinman," she said. The man's eyes flicked to the plastic card and then back to her face.

"Your ACIN number?"

"Two-four-eight-seven."

The man double checked, and then seemed satisfied. He saluted. "You're to come with me, Ms Steinman. Your father is aboard an aircraft carrier off Norfolk. He's been expecting you."

The helmeted man took a grip of Jessica's arm and hustled her from the car. I stared numbly, watching her scurry away towards the helicopter. She was shouting frantically up into the man's face, and then suddenly she tore free from his grip and scampered back towards me. She flung open the passenger door and I felt myself slumping heavily.

"He comes too!" I heard her shout.

"Only authorized personnel," the pilot shouted back. "I have strict orders."

"He is authorized," Jessica's voice became insistent and authoritative – a tone I'd never heard from her until this moment. "He's my White House bodyguard."

I felt gentle hands lift me from the car – big strong hands – that carried me to the helicopter. Then more hands heaved me aboard and laid me out on the cold steel floor as the two armed troopers clambered back aboard the helicopter, their guns still aimed guardedly back along the road. There was flurry of activity, an urgent shout of voices, and then another man's face hovered close mine, his brow furrowed, his expression sympathetic and kindly.

"You'll make it," the man said.

He had an oxygen mask in his hand and I saw it closing over my nose and mouth, but not before I heard Jessica Steinman's voice once more, even louder than the drumming rotors.

"Please take care of him," she said. "His name is Colin. Colin Walker. He saved my life."

The End.

Also available by Nicholas Ryan
Ground Zero: A Zombie Apocalypse

"Nicholas Ryan has delivered complete madness. A bloody zombie-smash from start to finish. Any fan of the genre will have a blast reading this."
- D.J. MOLLES
Bestselling Author of
'The Remaining', 'The Remaining: Aftermath', 'The Remaining: Refugees', 'The Remaining: Fractured'

Aboard a freighter bound for Baltimore harbor, an Iranian terrorist prepares to unleash an unimaginable horror upon the United States. The 'Wrath' is an undead plague - an infection that consumes its victims with a maddening rage and turns them into mindless blood-thirsty killers.
Jack Cutter is just an ordinary guy dealing with a dreadful guilt when the virus tears through his home town. Before it's too late, Cutter will have to find a way to survive, and find a reason to fight: HIS REDEMPTION.

A review from **Little Blog of Horror**

"When I think *zombie novels*, I used to think *Max Brooks*, but there is a new name I will think of from now on, **Nicholas Ryan**.
Many zombie novels that I have read have been severely lacking the proper descriptiveness to draw the reader into the horror they are trying to give them. **Nicholas Ryan's '*Ground Zero*** is every bit as *horrifying* and descriptive as a *Max*

Brooks novel. The scenes he describes are *terrifying* and so *vivid* I almost feel like I am watching a *George A. Romero* film. The way he depicts his characters and the scenarios that they are faced with, I could feel their *fear* and I felt as though I was watching all of these horrors unfold through the eyes of these terrified people. He gave every character a back story, so you really get to know them and learn what makes them tick. This is what makes any story worth reading.

The twists and turns that his main character, *Jack Cutter*, faces are fantastically thought out. The changes he goes through and the things he comes to terms with are both *heartbreaking* and *unsettling.*

'*Ground Zero'* is not a lengthy story, but packs all the punches of a *Stephen King* length novel. None of the story feels rushed. The natural flow of the novel from beginning to end is seamless and well thought out. Through the time that I was reading it, I never thought "*well this could be better*" or "*he really should have added something here*". '***Ground Zero'*** really is a work of art and has all of the makings of a real **horror literary classic**.

I could not recommend '*Ground Zero'* enough to anyone that enjoys a truly captivating horror story. Even if you are not a fan of horror or *zombie novels*, I would still give it a read.

12276084R00145

Made in the USA
San Bernardino, CA
16 June 2014